"If all you want is an appointment, we can meet at my agent's office tomorrow afternoon."

His hand fell away and he shoved it back into his pocket.

She stared at him, astonished, not only th___ was taking her deception so well, but that he ___ ave been expecting it. Then the kno___ ___ and she grinned, giddy ___ was. He knew why she w___ ___ her name after all fro___ ___ his agent and his pub___

"If, on the other hand___ ___, he continued, and giddy relief turr___ ___ ody shock, "then I'm happy to explore how much more. Tonight." His rough palm cupped her cheek, the husky tone of voice making the erotic intent unmistakable. "But whatever we do tonight has no bearing on what happens tomorrow. I don't do favors for sex." The light tone made the implication that she might have been suggesting such a thing seem amusing rather than insulting. "Even really good sex."

"What if it's not really good sex?" she asked, the question popping out before she could stop it.

His brows flew up and he choked out a laugh. A hot flush fired into her cheeks.

Good grief, Eva, shut up. It's not as if you're actually going to take him up on his offer.

But then he brushed the calloused skin of his thumb across her bottom lip. And every single reason that she couldn't possibly allow herself to be seduced by a man as dangerous as Nick Delisantro flew right out of her head.

HEIDI RICE was born and bred and still lives in London, England. She has two boys who love to bicker; a wonderful husband who, luckily for everyone, has loads of patience; and a supportive and ever-growing British/French/Irish/American family. As much as Heidi adores "the Big Smoke," she also loves America, and every two years or so she and her best friend leave hubby and kids behind and Thelma-and-Louise it across the States for a couple of weeks (although they always leave out the driving off a cliff bit). She's been a film buff since her early teens and a romance junkie for almost as long. She indulged her first love by being a film reviewer. Then a few years ago she decided to spice up her life by writing romance. Discovering the fantastic sisterhood of romance writers (both published and unpublished) in Britain and America made it a wild and wonderful journey to her first Mills & Boon® novel.

Heidi loves to hear from readers—you can email her at heidi@heidi-rice.com or visit her website, www.heidi-rice.com.

Other titles by Heidi Rice available in eBook

Harlequin Presents® Extra

THE GOOD, THE BAD AND THE WILD

HEIDI RICE

~ How to Flirt in Italian ~

TORONTO NEW YORK LONDON
AMSTERDAM PARIS SYDNEY HAMBURG
STOCKHOLM ATHENS TOKYO MILAN MADRID
PRAGUE WARSAW BUDAPEST AUCKLAND

Recycling programs
for this product may
not exist in your area.

ISBN-13: 978-0-373-52876-9

THE GOOD, THE BAD AND THE WILD

Copyright © 2012 by Heidi Rice

Printed in U.S.A.

THE GOOD, THE BAD AND THE WILD

To Abby Green for seeing me to the end of this book, and being a fabulous roomie in NYC 2011!

With special thanks to Michelle Styles, who knows the Bay Area much better than I do.

CHAPTER ONE

'Don't look now, but he's here and he's right behind us.'

Eva Redmond's heart catapulted into her throat as the urgent whisper from her old college chum Tess sliced through the hum of polite conversation and the tinkle of champagne glasses in the upscale San Francisco art gallery. 'Are you sure?'

Tess looked past Eva's right shoulder. 'Tall? Check.' She nodded. 'Dark? Check. Handsome? Check. The only one not in a suit? Check.' She grinned at Eva. 'Yup, it's definitely your rebel scriptwriter.' Her gaze flicked past Eva again. 'And you're in luck. Not only is he alone. But he's even hotter than his photo.'

Eva stared blankly at the six foot square canvas in front of her—which was titled The Explosion of the Senses, but looked more like an explosion in a paint factory to her untrained eye—and swallowed down the knot of apprehension that had been tightening around her larynx ever since she'd boarded the plane at Heathrow that morning.

The knowledge that the man she'd travelled five thousand miles to meet was standing a few feet away made it feel as if she were trying to swallow a boulder.

'Goodie,' she muttered.

Tess laughed and nudged her. 'Don't sound so pleased.'

'Why would I be pleased?' Eva whispered back, fairly sure

Nick Delisantro's extreme hotness was not going to work in her favour. If only he were a geeky academic. Sticking with what you knew might be dull. But dull had its advantages.

'Why wouldn't you be?' Tess countered. 'Giving a scorching hot guy the news that he's the heir to a fortune in Italian real estate is what I'd call a win-win situation.'

Eva nobly resisted the urge to sneak a peek over her shoulder. 'Yes, but I'm not you, am I?' she remarked wryly as she studied her friend dispassionately.

In her ice-blue, off the shoulder silk gown and six-inch designer heels, Tess looked elegant, slim, super-confident—and completely at home in the rarefied atmosphere of a gallery opening in San Francisco's Union Square neighbourhood. Which wasn't at all surprising. Tess had spent the last three years building a formidable reputation as an events planner in the US and even at university she'd been able to schmooze for England. Eva meanwhile had spent the years since she'd gained her first at Cambridge burying her nose in dusty antiquarian documents and computer research data. She couldn't schmooze to save her life—and she'd never felt more out of place than among all these beautiful people who had elevated socialising to an art form.

The admission touched some lonely place deep inside. She shook off the thought. She wasn't lonely; her life was exactly how she wanted it. Settled, secure, content. Until two days ago, when her boss Henry Crenshawe had demanded she travel halfway round the globe to be humiliated in public.

'And it's not as simple as telling him he could be the Duca D'Alegria's grandson. I'll also have to tell him the man he always thought was his biological father isn't.' Eva tensed at the thought of having such an intimate conversation with a stranger. A scorching hot stranger who had steadfastly ignored all her attempts to contact him in close to a month. 'I shouldn't have let you talk me into asking him for an appointment here. It's not appropriate.'

Tess gave an easy shrug. 'So don't ask him straight away. Flirt with him first. He'll be much more amenable. I guarantee it.'

Eva doubted that. She didn't know how to flirt and this man was a master at it. During her extensive research for the firm's high-profile new client, it was one of the few things she'd managed to discover about the elusive Niccolo Carmine Delisantro—the man who she had deduced was almost certainly the illegitimate grandson Don Vincenzo Palatino Vittorio Savargo De Rossi, the Duca D'Alegria, was offering a small fortune to locate.

The dry facts of Delisantro's life had told her very little about him as a person—North London runaway turned successful Hollywood scriptwriter and San Francisco resident who had scripted the biggest box-office hit of the decade five years ago—except that he was a wow with the ladies and he guarded his privacy like a hawk.

'You can take a look now, and see what you're up against.' Tess indicated with her champagne flute. 'Kate Elmsly's cornered him,' she finished, mentioning the perky and persistent gallery owner who had greeted them both earlier.

Trying to even her breathing, Eva turned. And her lungs seized to a halt. The back of her neck bristled as she took a hasty sip of her champagne cocktail. This was worse than she thought.

As she studied the man standing about ten feet away Eva realised she wasn't just out of her depth, she was in danger of drowning.

Tess was right. The grainy photo she'd managed to find on the Internet didn't do Nick Delisantro justice.

No mere human being had a right to that level of perfection. Thick wavy hair the colour of rich caramel curled to touch the collar of a worn black leather bomber jacket, which matched his thin black sweater and jeans. Sharp angular cheekbones with a hint of stubble, tanned olive skin to highlight his Italian heritage and a honed, muscular six foot plus physique combined to set him apart from the pampered crowd of local celebrities and dignitaries. His dark brooding masculine beauty drew female eyes, and hers were no exception—the relaxed, almost insolent way he leaned against the bare brick column as the gallery owner chatted effusively only made him seem more aloof. Surly, sexy, supremely magnetic, effortlessly successful as a hunter-gatherer but with a dangerous edge, Nick Delisantro was the perfect male prototype to ensure the survival of his species.

Eva sighed, a shiver running down her spine then sprinting straight back up again. While she was the female prototype to ensure it failed. An academic whose knowledge of men and sex included a few fumbled encounters as a post-grad and a secret passion for florid historical romance novels that had half-naked men with exceptional pecs on the covers.

She swung back to face 'The Explosion of the Senses,' her own senses imploding as her gaze skimmed down the designer gown Tess had lent her. 'This isn't going to work,' she murmured, more to herself than her friend. 'I look ridiculous.'

The crimson velvet creation with its split skirt and plunging neckline would look sensational on her friend, but Eva was two inches shorter and had several extra inches round the bust. The gown had made her feel exhilarated when she'd squeezed into it an hour ago, but now only made her feel like more of a fraud.

She wasn't one of those stunning damsels in distress with long flowing tresses and enough spirit to bring a marauding pirate captain to his knees. She was a risk-averse academic with a wardrobe full of beige who was still technically speaking a virgin at the ripe old age of twenty-four.

Tess placed a comforting hand on Eva's forearm. 'You do not look ridiculous. You look voluptuous.'

Eva crossed her arms over her chest. 'Flashing my boobs at him is not the way to go here,' she said, feeling more uncomfortable by the second. 'I should just go to his agent's office tomorrow morning and ask him for an appointment.' That would be the safe, smart thing to do, and had been Eva's plan all along until Tess had discovered through her many contacts that Nick Delisantro was attending tonight's gala opening and wheedled them both an invite.

'Cleavage is never a bad thing where men are concerned,' Tess asserted. 'And you said this commission is important,' she urged. 'If his agent blows you off, what are you going to tell your boss?'

Eva didn't have an answer for that. Mr Crenshawe had told her in no uncertain terms that Roots Registry valued the De Rossi commission, and if Eva delivered the missing heir before one of the rival companies the duca had hired located him too, she would finally be in line for a promotion.

It was a powerful incentive. Eva adored her job. Poring over diaries and journals and correlating the evidence left by birth, marriage and death certificates allowed her to imagine lives often lived centuries ago—their passions, their pain, their triumphs and tragedies. And the promotion she'd worked so hard for would finally give her the job security she craved.

Tess craned her neck to peer past Eva. 'It looks like he's shaken off Kate,' she continued. 'Go now.' She prodded Eva with her elbow. 'Brush past him on your way to the bar. The dress will do the rest.'

'And if it doesn't?' Eva asked tentatively, not sure the revealing dress was something she could actually control.

Tess shrugged. 'Then you haven't lost a thing. We'll go back to my place and you can try out plan B for Boring tomorrow.'

'Okay.' Eva took a shuddering breath, feeling as if she were about to walk the plank—in nothing but her underwear. 'I'll walk past him on my way to the toilet.' How hard could that be? 'But then we're leaving.'

She handed Tess her empty champagne flute and smoothed

shaky palms down the luxurious velvet. The soft, seductive material brushed against her thighs as she concentrated on not falling flat on her face in the unfamiliar four-inch heels she'd also borrowed from Tess. She glanced towards him as she drew level, positive he wouldn't even have noticed her. And froze.

Heavy lidded chocolate eyes, as bold and insolent as the rest of him, caught hers and held. The image of Rafe, the pirate captain from her favourite, much-thumbed novel, shimmered like a mirage then cleared. A shaky breath gushed out as she stared back, transfixed by the way the overhead light caught the golden flecks in his irises. The colour was unusually striking and very familiar. She'd seen the exact same shade when the duca had arrived at their offices in London to hand over his dead son's journal.

His grandson's lips lifted a fraction on one side, as if he were enjoying a private joke, then his gaze dipped. Eva's heart punched her ribcage with the force of a heavyweight champ.

The lazy perusal raked over her sensitised skin like a physical caress, before his gaze met hers again. 'Do I know you?' he asked, the tone husky and amused, curt British vowels laced with the hint of a Californian drawl.

Eva shook her head, her tongue apparently stapled to the roof of her mouth.

'So why have you and your friend been spying on me?' he asked.

Good Lord, he has bionic hearing.

Eva's breathing choked to a stop. Then released in a rush as her common sense caught up with the kick of panic. He couldn't possibly have heard them—with all the hard surfaces the noise level in the gallery was loud and discordant. He must have spotted Tess watching him. Tess wasn't exactly subtle.

'We couldn't help it,' she said, trying to think of a viable excuse. 'You're a lot more intriguing than the art.'

'Is that right?' One brow lifted, making her breathing accelerate. 'I'm not sure that's a compliment. A daytime soap would be more intriguing than this stuff.' The disdainful comment was belied by the wry tone. 'What's so intriguing about me?'

Eva's breathing slowed and she began to get a little lightheaded.

Was he flirting with her?

'You don't belong here,' she stammered, the fierce buzz of anticipation in her stomach coming from nowhere. 'But you don't care. That's unusual in a social situation. The normal response is to want to participate. To be part of the crowd. That makes you intriguing.'

The words trailed off as his lips quirked in a curious grin, softening his angular features.

Stop lecturing, you idiot. You sound like a professor.

He straightened away from the column, making her aware that he was at least half a foot taller than her, even in her borrowed heels.

Lifting his arm, he propped it against the column, angling his body so he shielded them both from the rest of the gallery. He stood close enough for her to smell the tantalising musk of soap and leather and pheromones. And see the crescent shaped scar drawing a white line through the shadow of stubble on his cheek. The pirate fantasy flickered at the edges of her consciousness. She forced it back, but not before the pulse of heat rippled over her skin and made her heart rate shoot back up to warp speed.

'You worked all that out after a few minutes?' he drawled.

Guilt tightened the muscles in her throat.

Not exactly.

'That's what I do. I'm an anthropologist.' *Of sorts.* 'I study people and their behaviour patterns. How they interact socially and culturally.' It wasn't exactly a lie, and she had a BSc to prove it.

'An anthropologist,' he said, savouring the word as if it

were a rare single malt whisky. His gaze roamed over her, and her nipples squeezed into hard, aching points. 'I've never met an anthropologist before.'

And he wasn't meeting one now, she thought, her gaze flicking away from his. This was the perfect time to tell him the truth—that she was the woman whose phone calls and email messages he'd refused to return for three and a half weeks. But instead of seizing the opportunity to get down to the business of begging him for an appointment, the butterflies already fluttering in her stomach went AWOL, and she hesitated.

She'd never had the chance to flirt with a man like this before. Never been studied in that frank, assessing way, the pulse of awareness arching between them more potent than any drug.

'Anthropology can be fascinating,' she heard herself murmur, feeling inexplicably needy.

'I'll bet,' he said. 'Although you're wrong about me.' His gaze drifted over her hair, which Tess had spent an hour taming into a chignon. 'I belong here just fine.' Lowering his arm, he hooked one of the stray curls that had fallen out of the chignon. 'But you, on the other hand, don't belong at all.' The back of his finger brushed her cheek, the touch subtle but so unexpected, she jumped.

He chuckled. 'What are you afraid of?'

You.

Heat pulsed in that secret place between her thighs at the intimate question. She wasn't afraid of him, that would be ludicrous, it was just that she'd never been touched like that before, with a sense of entitlement.

'I'm not afraid,' she blurted out, the urge to run sudden and instinctive and oddly intoxicating. 'I have to go to the rest room.'

He tucked the lock of hair behind her ear with a care that

made her heart throb in unison with her pulse points. 'Let's discuss anthropology when you get back.'

The suggestion was casual but proprietary and only disturbed her more. She might be a novice at this, but she didn't think this conversation had anything to do with anthropology any more.

Giving a non-committal nod, she rushed away, sure she could feel his golden gaze boring into the bare skin of her back—with the patient, predatory instincts of a lion hunting a gazelle.

The preposterous image made her breath catch. She had to get out of here—before she completely lost her grip on sanity. Plan B for Boring would have to do, because Plan A was way too terrifying—and exciting.

Colour me amazed.

Nick huffed out a rough chuckle as he watched the sexy anthropologist dash through the crowd and admired the swing of her hips in the stop-light red dress.

When was the last time he'd met someone so intriguing, especially at one of these tedious social functions?

He'd have to send Jay, his publicist, a thank you note for insisting that he venture away from his laptop tonight. Except that he hadn't really attended the gallery opening at Jay's insistence, but out of sheer boredom having spent the day staring at a screen full of rubbish.

Leaning back against the column, he closed his eyes, shutting out the hum of inane chatter and hoping to deter anyone from approaching him while he waited for the Woman in Red's return.

She'd captivated him, which was surprising in itself. He didn't appreciate being watched or whispered about, and he'd spotted her and her friend doing exactly that. But there was something about the way she had peered at him, with none of the usual calculation or confidence he had come to expect from the women that approached him. And then when he'd got a better look at her, his senses had kicked into overdrive like those of a hormonally charged teenager.

He kept his lids closed, picturing her, and tried to determine the trigger. Creamy, translucent skin? Wide blue eyes so dark they were almost violet? The flutter of her pulse visible in the graceful arch of her collarbone? Russet curls that had escaped the mass of hair artfully piled on her head? The swell of her breasts revealed by the plunging neckline of her gown? The fresh, simple scent of soap and spring flowers? The crisp, precise London accent that he hadn't heard in years?

Any one of those things could have turned him on. He was a guy after all. But still, she wasn't conventionally beautiful: not particularly tall; her eyes had been maybe too big, she had a slight overbite and her forthright observations about his character had unsettled him. Even though they could only have been a lucky guess.

Weird? There was no explaining the ferocity of attraction. Not really. Except maybe…?

He opened his eyes, found himself shifting round to look at the doors to the rest room.

And realised that by far the most captivating thing about her had been her unguarded response. Her breathing had quickened, her pupils dilating wildly as soon as she stopped in front of him. The truth was he'd always been jaded where women were concerned. Even as a boy. Once he'd grown up, he found himself craving sex as much as any man, but for him it had never been more than a physical release. And as a result in the last few years, ever since *The Deadly Touch* had made him one of the hottest properties in Hollywood, he'd developed a cynicism about the women he dated that meant while sex was satisfying, it had become less and less exciting.

He knew precisely which buttons to press to get the response from women he wanted. But when was the last time a woman had responded to him so instinctively—and with so little caution? She'd been so transparent, the instant physical connection between them so intense, he was sure it had to be an act. But act or not, he was still captivated. And intrigued. It was certainly a very long time since he'd felt this level of attraction. He glanced round, smiling at his own impatience, then pushed away from the column as he spotted her standing by the rest-room doors, talking into her cell phone. Not talking, pleading by the look of it. She snapped the phone closed, stuffed it into her purse, then rushed out of the back entrance of the gallery.

He was so astonished, it took him a moment to figure out that she'd left. Acting on impulse, he charged after her, snaking his way through the crowd.

Where the hell was she off to in such a hurry? He didn't even know her name. And he wasn't finished with her yet. Not by a long shot.

CHAPTER TWO

'Hey, wait up.'

Eva's head whipped round at the shout from behind her. She skidded to a halt, stumbling as she recognised the tall silhouette backlit by the light from the open doorway.

Strong fingers grasped her arm, steadying her. 'You okay?'

The firedoor crashed shut, throwing the alleyway into shadow.

'Yes,' she murmured, cursing the guilty blush burning her neck. 'Thank you. I'm not used to these heels.'

His fingers stroked down her arm, setting off a series of lightning bolts, before he let her go. 'I always wonder why women wear those ankle-breakers.'

'To make our legs look longer.'

He gave a gruff chuckle, the sound strangely intimate in the darkness. 'Is that so?' She saw his head dip as her eyes adapted to the low light. She took a staggered breath and his tantalising scent engulfed her, masking the aroma of wet pavements and disinfectant.

'You don't need any help on that score,' he remarked, his voice low and amused.

She wrapped her arms around herself, the chilled autumn air not the only thing causing her goosebumps. Was he flirting with her again? Why had he followed her? And why was his attention as intoxicating as it was terrifying?

'I suppose you're right,' she said. 'Given that broken ankles are even less attractive than short legs.'

He laughed again, the rough murmur chasing the blush into her cheeks.

Stop being so literal, you muppet.

'Where are you going?' he asked, mercifully ignoring her pathetic attempts at conversation.

'I…' She choked to a stop. She didn't have an answer. Her instinctive need to flee from him seeming even more ridiculous than her small talk. 'I wanted some fresh air. It's stuffy in there,' she lied.

Unfortunately, the lie didn't quite come off when she shivered.

'You're cold.' Shrugging off his jacket, he lifted her bag off her shoulder. 'Here.' Warm leather surrounded her. His scent clung to the garment, and she had to purse her lips to stop from sighing.

'Let's go for a ride.'

'I beg your pardon?' she stammered, the tone of his voice making all sorts of inappropriate, but far too appealing, thoughts pop into her mind.

'A ride.' He buried his hands in his back pockets, hunched against the cold in the crew-neck sweater and nodded down the alleyway. 'I've got my bike round the corner. And I was looking for an excuse to escape myself.'

'You mean a motorbike?'

Placing a warm palm on the small of her back, he directed her towards the end of the alleyway, subtly leading her in the direction he wanted to go. 'It's a great way to see the city. You're a Londoner, right? Like me.'

'Um, yes,' she said, dazed by the little sizzles of electrical energy where his palm rested on her lower back.

'So when did you arrive?'

'I…' She paused. She should tell him now. But her tongue

seemed to get stuck in neutral again. 'This afternoon. I'm visiting my friend Tess.'

'The other nosey one?'

She gave a nervous laugh. 'Yes, sorry.'

'Don't be,' he said as they drew level with a monstrous black motorbike, its swirling logo and silver trim gleaming dangerously in the street lamp light. 'I like getting talked about by beautiful women.'

'Oh,' she said, not sure how to take the compliment. Was he trying to be funny? She looked good tonight, but no one would mistake her for beautiful, not unless they were seriously myopic.

Unlocking the box at the back of the bike, he lifted out a helmet. 'Put this on.'

She took the helmet without thinking. Standing dumbfounded as he mounted the huge machine with easy grace.

He glanced back at her. 'Hop on.'

'But I'm wearing a dress,' she said, struggling to slow things down a little. She'd never been on a motorbike before, especially not with a man of his... Power. 'And heels,' she added. 'What if I fall off?'

Placing a proprietary hand on her hip, he nudged her round to face him, took the helmet from her, and plopped it on her head. 'You won't.' He tucked the tendrils of hair into the helmet with a focused concentration that had her pulse throbbing in her throat. 'Not as long as you hold on tight.'

Fastening the helmet's strap, he ran his thumb across her chin. The tiny touch made her shiver and her tongue slipped out of its own accord, licking lips that had gone dry as a desert.

His gaze dipped and she pressed her lips together, the buzz of anticipation almost unbearable. When his eyes lifted back to her face, she could see amusement. And a disturbing intensity.

'Where do you want to go?' he murmured.

Anywhere you want to take me.

She slammed down on the impulsive thought and the much more impulsive thrum of tension that had her whole body vibrating.

She shouldn't be doing this. It wasn't just impulsive, it was reckless—bordering on inappropriate. And she'd never done anything before that bordered on reckless, let alone inappropriate.

But maybe that was exactly the problem, she realised, as the thrum of tension refused to subside. In that split second of indecision, her whole well-ordered and completely appropriate life seemed to stretch out before her in a rolling canvas of total and extreme boredom and the impulsiveness took hold of her tongue.

'I don't know. You decide,' she said, the whispered words so liberating she heard a strange sound come out of her mouth, which sounded suspiciously like a giggle.

Niccolo Delisantro chuckled back. 'See, that wasn't so hard,' he said, with surprising intuition.

Eva stiffened. Did he know how big a deal this was for her? That adventures were something she'd only ever read about in books? That her life was about as dynamic as magnolia wallpaper?

'Climb aboard and let's get this show on the road,' he added, and she shook off the humiliating thought. How could he know? He didn't know the first thing about her.

She stifled the little pang of guilt at the thought of how much she knew about him. As soon as the ride was over, she'd tell him who she was. And face the consequences. But just this once, she wanted to give in to impulse.

She adjusted the helmet on her head, then hesitated, studying the enormous machine and the small segment of leather seat available to her.

Adventure was one thing, but how on earth did you climb

onto a motorbike that large? In four-inch heels and a figure-hugging designer dress?

He stood up to stamp on one of the pedals and the monster roared to life. She jumped at the explosion of sound.

'Um…I'm not sure how to…' She shouted above the engine noise. 'How do I…?' He adjusted his wrist and the noise subsided to a dull rumble. 'Do you have any instructions?'

The colour charged back into her cheeks at the easy grin he sent her over his shoulder.

So much for Eva Redmond, wild child. What kind of a loser asks for instructions on how to mount a motorbike?

Swivelling round, he lowered his gaze to her legs. 'I'm guessing you'll have to hike the skirt up.' The mischievous glint in his golden eyes made colour race over her scalp and stand the fine hair on the back of her neck on end. He leaned over and flipped open a short rubber pedal that stuck out above the gleaming silver exhaust pipe. 'Step on that and then take my arm.' So saying he held out his hand.

Biting into her bottom lip, she gathered the skirt clumsily up her legs. 'Here goes,' she mumbled as she gripped his arm. Feeling the muscles of his forearm tense, she slipped while placing her instep onto the pedal.

'Easy,' he soothed. 'There's no hurry.'

She gave him a hopeful smile, praying that her blush was dimmed somewhat by the low lighting and that she wasn't about to knock the two of them into a heap on the pavement. Then took a deep breath and launched her leg over the bike.

He gave a sharp tug as she did so, and she landed on the leather bench with a huff. Her breath sucked into her lungs at the sudden, explosive mix of sensations. The bike's heavy vibrations shuddered up through her backside, her nipples hardening into peaks as they touched the unyielding slopes of his back. The skin of her inner thighs sizzled alarmingly as the dress hitched up and she came into intimate contact with the rough denim of his jeans.

The tight muscular contours of his backside flexed through his clothing and the blush intensified.

Oh, God. She'd never been this close to a man before. Ever. The sensations racing through her were both exquisite and yet petrifying on some elemental level. She leaned back, worried he'd feel her nipples poking him, but that only intensified the pressure of his denim-clad butt pressing into her spread thighs. She fanned her hand in front of her face, convinced she was having her first hot flush thirty years too soon.

What had possessed her to agree to do this? What if she passed out from sensory overload and fell off the bike? Then got flattened by a cable car and ended up horribly mangled in the middle of a San Francisco street?

'Put your arms round my waist.' The rough command sliced neatly through her panic attack and she obeyed him instinctively. Circling him, she pressed her cheek against the silky smooth cashmere sweater and linked her fingers, trying desperately to ignore the tensile strength of his abdomen beneath her palms.

She squeezed her eyes shut as the bike jerked forward off its stand. He revved the engine, signalling another sensory overload as the shudder of leashed power made her pulse jump.

'Relax.' One large palm covered the back of her hands, still locked round his waist. 'You're safe. I swear.' She felt the rumble of his chuckle through her cheek and tried to loosen her death grip.

'My name's Nick, by the way,' he said, his warm palm letting go of her hands to steer the bike off the pavement and into the road with a jolt. 'Nick Delisantro. What's yours?'

'Eva,' she said, the renewed stab of guilt going some way to calming her rioting nervous system. 'Eva Redmond,' she added, then tensed at the realisation that he might well recognise her name and call a halt to the whole fiasco.

She frowned. The fact that she would be desperately disappointed if he did, despite the mix of terror and anticipation making her stomach churn, had to be yet more evidence that she was probably having some sort of weird emotional meltdown.

'Nice to meet you,' he said, clearly oblivious to her deception.

She breathed a ragged sigh. But as her cheek brushed the velvet steel of his back she made herself a solemn promise. She would definitely tell him who she was once their wild ride was over. No more evasions.

Assuming she survived her wild ride.

Her heartbeat slammed into her throat as the bike leapt forward like a savage beast, and reared away from the kerb. Eva's legs squeezed his backside while her arms tightened around his waist, her fingers clasped so tight she was in danger of dislocating a knuckle.

'Welcome to San Fransisco, Eva the anthropologist,' he shouted back at her.

More like Eva the Fraud.

The quick burst of shame did nothing to dim the heady kick of adrenaline as the bike tilted into a turn and then accelerated up the steep hill into the night.

Eva clung on tight and for the first time in her life allowed herself to rejoice in the thrill of doing something reckless. And unwise. And inappropriate.

And completely and utterly intoxicating.

Terror gave way to fascination as the scent of roasted duck and Szechuan spices made Eva's stomach rumble. She swivelled her head back and forth trying to take in the kaleidoscope of people as the bike wound through the traffic choked thoroughfare. The oriental faces and exotic hieroglyphics on the signs and posters marked the area out as Chinatown. But almost as soon as she had registered the fact, they took a sharp turn and left the crowded street behind. A cable car trundled past on the cross street in front of them, like something out of a bygone era, but for the tourists in shorts and T-shirts with cameras round their necks sandwiched onto the bench seats. Shuddering over the cable-car tracks, the bike climbed and dipped through hills of ornate Victorian town houses, stopping and starting on every corner. Eva's heart thumped against her chest wall, the emotion swelling in her throat at the overwhelming beauty of the city gilded by the dying sun.

She threw her head back, let the evening air brush a few escaped tendrils of hair against her cheeks.

Her eyes stung with tears. How could she have spent the first twenty-four years of her life never having done anything remotely spontaneous or daring?

Her parents had been in their fifties when they'd had her. Both of them brilliant academics dedicated to their chosen fields. When she'd been conceived by accident, they hadn't had a clue how to factor a child into their busy lives. So she'd adapted instead. Which had meant being cautious and responsible and respecting the boundaries they set, even when she was a teenager and every other person she knew was busy tearing them down.

No wonder she was such a coward.

But maybe adventure didn't always have to be bad. Or contained within the pages of the romance novels her parents had always insisted were 'a foolish indulgence'.

She blinked furiously and clung tighter as they edged down another steep incline. The man in front of her felt so solid, his broad back sheltering her from the lengthening shadows. Then the bike hit a major road. Suddenly they were leaving the picture-postcard houses, the steep slopes and stepped pavements behind. Trees and parklands sped past and then Eva gasped, her eyes widening in wonder as the Golden Gate Bridge reared up before them, a huge geometric monolith of rusty red steel lit by the dying sun.

The bike thundered through the fingers of fog drifting

over the road, the rush of air and noise both cold and thrilling as they zipped past the occasional car, and a monstrous shiny yellow eighteen-wheeler. Squeezing her eyes shut, Eva hugged the only still thing in her universe and felt them both take flight through the traffic, hurtling across the water. The ball of emotion broke lose. Firing up her torso, it burst out of her mouth and she let out a gleeful yell that whipped away on the wind.

She'd been walking through a fog her entire life but now the cloying veil of conformity was being ripped away—making every colour more vivid, every scent more acute, every sense more vibrant.

To think she had lived her whole life and never experienced anything as thrilling as a sunset ride across San Francisco Bay?

Adrenaline and affection blossomed as she clung to Nick Delisantro. How could she ever thank him enough, for giving her this?

CHAPTER THREE

As the bike wound through the nature reserve on the Marin headlands, taking the climb towards Hawk Hill, Nick glanced at the fingers knotted round his waist and smiled.

He'd hazard a guess that Eva the gorgeous anthropologist had never ridden pillion before, given the way she was attached to him like a limpet. Not that he was complaining. Once she'd got the hang of leaning into the turns, the feel of her clinging to him had been very nice indeed. Her shocked little gasp when they'd hit the Bridge on 101, and her spontaneous shout as they'd raced across it had only added to the heat. Seemed the prim and proper Miss Eva had a wild side. When you factored in the familiar adrenaline kick of being on the bike and the awe-inspiring view as they topped the rise and drifted to a stop at the overlook…

No, he definitely didn't have a single complaint about his split-second decision to invite her along. It had been far too long since he'd enjoyed the city like this—or the feel of a woman's soft, pliant body plastered against his.

He felt her expel another sharp breath as he cut off the bike's engine.

'Wow.' Her hushed murmur sent a delicious tingle through the short hairs at his nape. 'It's so beautiful.'

He tilted the bike onto its stand, flattened his feet onto the ground. 'Yeah. This is the best view of the bridge.'

They sat for a while in silence, admiring the majestic span of the Golden Gate, blazing a trail across the bay in the sunset, the fog sitting like a carpet of mist over the water and the lights of the city laid out behind.

Reluctantly, he placed a hand over hers, glanced round at wind-stung cheeks and wide violet eyes. 'It's safe to let go now.'

Pulling her hands out from under his, she sprang back. 'I'm so sorry. Was I holding on too tight?'

Her cheeks flushed a becoming shade of pink, and, despite the camouflage of his leather jacket, he caught a tantalising glimpse of her cleavage.

With a figure like that she couldn't possibly be as innocent as she seemed. Guys would have been all over her since puberty. But it was still an intriguing act.

'You've my permission to hold on as tight as you like,' he murmured. 'But if you want to stretch your legs for a minute and enjoy the view…'

'Yes…Thank you, I would,' she said in that very proper London accent, but didn't budge.

He waited a beat. 'You'll have to dismount first,' he prompted, stifling a grin when the colour highlighting her cheekbones flared again in the fading light.

'Oh, yes, of course.' Shifting back on the seat, she gathered her dress and then bit into her bottom lip as she concentrated on her dismount. It took a moment for her to execute the manoeuvre, during which he got an eyeful of lush thighs and trim calves displayed in silky nylons. He held back a groan, the clumsiness of her dismount making the view even more enticing as her many curves jiggled. Clearly it had been far too long since he'd had that much lush, scented female flesh within touching distance.

Swinging his leg over the bike, he stood behind her as she lifted the helmet off. With her back to him as she gazed out across the city, the top of her head barely reached his chin. Curls of reddish-brown hair, no longer contained by the arrangement at the top, fell in disarray around the graceful column of her neck. Would her hair look all soft and rumpled like that straight out of bed? He stepped close enough to hear the staggered rise and fall of her breathing and to catch a whiff of her through the scent of sea-salt and earth. Spring flowers and soap, the fresh, unsophisticated scent seemed somehow exotic. He wanted to caress the back of her neck so badly he could almost feel her skin against his fingertips.

Burying his hands into the back pockets of his jeans, he tried to recall for about the fiftieth time since he'd spotted her in the gallery why he'd sworn off romantic entanglements a few months ago. Something to do with a script that wasn't happening, a looming production deadline and the unpleasant scenes when Lisa, his last girlfriend, had finally figured out that he'd meant it when he'd told her he wasn't *that* interested in her. But as the once convincing reasons swirled through his mind again, they didn't stop the urge to reach out and touch.

'It's really an astonishing feat of structural engineering,' she said.

'Uh-huh,' he replied. Although it wasn't the bridge's astonishing feats of engineering that he was admiring at the moment.

He caught the words 'truss arches' and 'cantilevered suspension' as she continued to talk, the words rushing out as if she'd swallowed an architectural textbook, and he found the grin tugging at his mouth again. He'd crashed out of school at sixteen and never gone back, so why did he find that serious, studious tone so damn sexy? He let his gaze drift down to the round swell of her backside lovingly spotlit by the bike's headlamp in rich red velvet—and decided maybe it wasn't so much the tone, but the contrasting packaging that was so appealing.

As the four-syllable words continued to tumble out she hugged the helmet to her midriff like a long-lost child. She was nervous. The thought added a nice little ego-boost to his attraction. It was kind of intoxicating to get the chance to do the chasing for a change.

As he waited patiently for her to wind down and look at him, something he suspected her lecture on the Golden Gate Bridge was being used to avoid, he pulled one hand out of his pocket.

Time to refocus her attention.

Angling his thumb under the line of dangling curls, he skimmed it across the whisper-soft skin of her neck just above the collar of his jacket.

The lecture cut off and she shot round, her eyes fixing on him at last, her skin pale in the light from the bike's head-lamps.

He smiled. She couldn't have looked more shocked if he had poked her with a cattle prod. He held out his hand, his thumb still tingling from the subtle contact. 'You want to give me the helmet? I'll stick it on the bike.'

She glanced at the helmet, as if she'd forgotten it. She re-laxed her hold, and those amazing violet eyes met his again. 'Thank you,' she said, passing it to him.

He walked the few steps to the bike and fixed it to the handlebar.

'Sorry,' she said again when he turned back to her. 'I talk too much.' She looked away. 'I just…' Even white teeth worried her bottom lip and he imagined nipping at the plump flesh and then gliding his tongue across to lick it better. 'I read an article about the bridge's construction in the in-flight magazine. It was fascinating.'

'It's a cool bridge,' he agreed, letting his gaze linger on her lips. Her bottom lip trembled and then her tongue flicked out to moisten it. The answering jolt of heat hit his groin like an Exocet missile.

His eyes locked on hers as he let out a strained laugh. 'But right now, I'm finding you a lot more fascinating.'

'I...' Eva clamped her mouth shut, before she swallowed her tongue. Or, worse, started spewing loads more twaddle about the Golden Gate Bridge like an overzealous tour guide.

His eyes took another leisurely trip down to her toes and she clasped her arms harder around her midriff, the worn leather of his jacket offering very little protection from the zip and zing of awareness.

Ever since he'd brushed his finger across her nape, she felt as if she'd been wired up to a nuclear reactor. And everywhere his gaze wandered felt as if it were being zapped with several billion kilowatts of energy.

She'd always adored reading about the instant overpowering sexual chemistry between the bold heroines and the impossibly masculine heroes in her favourite romances. But she'd never believed it actually existed in real life. Had simply assumed it was as fictional as all the hyper-real emotions and lavish derring-do. After all, none of her kind and conscientious male colleagues, or Phil, the chess club president she'd dated briefly in college without getting past second base, had ever made her giddy. Her physical reaction to Nick Delisantro, however, was forcing her to reconsider, because it felt every bit as out of control and extraordinary as the most fantastical romantic fantasy.

All this man had to do was look at her, his heavy-lidded eyes dark with erotic promise and warmth flooded every single cell of her body. The skin of her nape was still tingling from the barely there brush of his fingertip, for goodness sake.

She let out a shuddering sigh as she curled her toes in the ankle-breaking heels, forcing herself to meet his gaze. 'You must be easily fascinated.'

He cocked his head, observing her with nerve-racking intensity. 'Not true.' His lips quirked. 'If you knew me better, you'd know I'm next to impossible to fascinate.'

She pushed out a little laugh, guilty knowledge tying her stomach in knots. She wondered how fascinated he would be if he knew the truth. That underneath the glamorous camouflage of Tess's designer dress lurked dull and dependable Eva Redmond?

'I do know who you are,' she said, quelling the dreadful stab of disappointment. 'Our meeting tonight wasn't an accident. I've been trying to contact you for over three weeks to make an appointment with you.' The twist of curiosity on his lips died. 'I went to that gallery opening tonight because it's imperative that I speak to you about—'

He touched his finger to her mouth, silencing her confession. 'Shh.' To her amazement his lips curved in a wry smile. 'I get it.' He shrugged. 'If all you want is an appointment, we can meet at my agent's office tomorrow afternoon.' His hand fell away and he shoved it back in his pocket.

She stared at him, astonished, not only that he was taking her deception so well, but that he seemed to have been expecting it. Then the greasy knots of tension dissolved and she grinned, giddy with relief. He knew who she was. He knew why she was here. He must have recognised her name after all from all the messages she'd left with his agent and his publicist.

'If, on the other hand, you want more,' he continued, and giddy relief turned to giddy shock, 'then I'm happy to explore how much more. Tonight.' His rough palm cupped her cheek, the husky tone of voice making the erotic intent unmistakeable. 'But whatever we do tonight has no bearing on what happens tomorrow. I don't do favours for sex.' The light tone made the implication that she might have been suggesting such a thing seem amusing rather than insulting. 'Even really good sex.'

'What if it's not really good sex?' she asked, the question popping out before she could stop it.

His brows flew up and he choked out a laugh. A hot flush fired into her cheeks.

Good grief, Eva, shut up. It's not like you're actually going to take him up on his offer.

But then he brushed the callused skin of his thumb across her bottom lip. And every single reason why she couldn't possibly allow herself to be seduced by a man as dangerous as Nick Delisantro flew right out of her head.

'Why don't you let me worry about that?' he murmured.

She sucked in a breath, the throb of heat between her thighs painful.

Kiss me.

The words echoed in her mind. But his gaze flared, as if he had heard her plea and he leaned close, surrounding her in his spicy scent, then pressed firm lips to hers. She let out a staggered breath, the contact as unexpected as having the silent yearning instantly fulfilled.

His tongue traced her bottom lip then explored in expert strokes, his hand capturing her head. She opened her mouth to let him in, her palms flattening against his chest, fingers clutching at the soft wool of his sweater as heat sizzled across her skin. Her tongue delved back, timid at first, then growing in confidence, coaxed into action by the warm, wet skill of his lips, his tongue.

The kiss seemed to go on for an eternity, and yet ended too soon.

He lifted his head, those golden eyes locked on hers. Her breathing rasped, her heartbeat hammered, the frantic pounding drowning out the distant hum of passing traffic, the keening cry of a bird of prey.

'You taste good,' he said, before nipping at her bottom lip.

'So do you,' she replied, mesmerised.

A drop of water splashed on her cheek and she jumped.

'Damn,' he cursed softly, brushing the rain off her cheek-bone with his thumb. He held his palm up to the sky. 'We better take this indoors. It's about to rain.' His eyes took on a feral gleam in the dark. 'You want to come back to mine?'

She knew what he was asking, knew what would happen if she took him up on the bold invitation. And knew at every other time in her life before now she would have refused. But the rebellious instinct that had made her climb on his bike and made her hoot for joy as they crossed the bridge geysered up inside her again, like a volcano of need forced to be dormant for far too long. And the refusal got stuck somewhere around her solar plexus.

Tomorrow she would meet him at his agent's office, give him the details of his inheritance and arrange his first contact with the Duca D'Alegria. Roots Registry would get their all-important commission, her promotion would be secure and she and Nick would never see each other again.

Nick Delisantro was *not* a tormented pirate captain about to forsake his wicked ways so he could declare his everlasting love. He was a flesh-and-blood man who was clearly exceptionally well adjusted to his wicked ways.

And she wasn't a gullible fool despite the guilty pleasure she took in reading larger-than-life romantic fantasies. She knew what Nick Delisantro was offering was strictly a one-night deal.

But why shouldn't she take that crazy leap into sexual fantasy and indulge in the heat of the moment, just for tonight?

She sucked in a calming breath. This was crazy thinking. Was she seriously considering racing headlong into bed with a man she barely knew?

Her breath gushed out and she heard herself say, ever so politely. 'I'd love to, thank you.'

That would be a yes, then.

The fierce arousal in his gaze was anything but polite as he nodded back. 'Great, let's go.'

He gripped her hand, hauling her towards the bike as she picked her way across the rocky ground in the heels.

The lights of the bridge blurred in the drizzle of autumn rain as the powerful machine lurched down the hill in the darkness. Eva's pulse lurched right along with it, the thunder of her heartbeat drowning out the engine's roar as she clung to her fantasy man and refused to contemplate the notion that she'd just made the most catastrophic mistake of her adult life.

CHAPTER FOUR

THE trip back sped past, despite the stop to pay a toll on the bridge, the bike travelling through a tunnel before emerging into parkland. The spitting rain hit Eva's cheeks, soaking her clothes as she huddled behind Nick's back and tried not to envision herself hurtling full pelt towards disaster.

It had taken her all her adult life to come into contact with someone as potent as Nick Delisantro. What if she had to wait another lifetime to meet someone this attractive again? This was a once-in-a-lifetime opportunity, which she refused to regret. At least until tomorrow.

Edging the park, they entered a neighbourhood decorated with psychedelic murals and scribbled graffiti. People in colourful slickers stood outside bars, defiantly smoking in the rain, while down-and-outs huddled in doorways and under awnings. Eva knew from her research that Nick lived in an area called Haight Ashbury, a place that had become famous during the Flower Power days of the late sixties. As they drifted past a cornucopia of hippie chic—from smoothie bars, to vegan cafés and a New Age market with a marijuana leaf logo and enough neon-coloured tie-dye clothing in the window to make your eyes bleed—Eva figured the Haight hadn't quite left the Summer of Love behind.

Turning off the main street, the bike rumbled to a stop on a wide tree-lined avenue in front of a five-storey Victorian terrace. Pale blue wooden siding, giant bay windows, elaborately carved trim and a stunning pergola at the top gave it a kitsch antique grandeur that wouldn't have looked out of place on Disneyland's Main Street.

Shifting round, Nick shouted, 'There's a gizmo in the jacket pocket. Give it a buzz.'

Finding the smooth plastic device, Eva pressed the button and a large door beneath the front steps lifted with an electric whine. Harsh neon lights flickered on as Nick drove the bike into a musty cellar garage. Shelves crowded with boxes lined one wall while a washing machine and drier stood in the opposite corner.

Eva clambered off the bike as the door whirred closed, but not before every one of the doubts that she'd been busy trying to pretend didn't exist sneaked in with her. She levered off the helmet. Her hair plopped onto her shoulders, the artfully arranged chignon now a mass of wet tangles. The velvet of Tess's beautiful dress clung to her thighs in sodden patches.

Inadequacy assailed her as she watched Nick dismount and shove the bike onto its stand. His tall physique only looked more spectacular in the soaking jeans and jumper. Spotlighted by the brittle white light, the denim moulded to long, lean thighs while damp cashmere clung to the sleek musculature of his chest and shoulders.

Maybe this hadn't been such an excellent idea after all. She looked about as sexy as a drowned collie while he looked like Adonis. Her stomach squeezed. Maybe she simply wasn't capable of being a bad girl, even for one night.

He disengaged the bike key and shoved it in his back pocket, then swiped his hair off his forehead. Drops of water dampened the concrete as she debated how best to decline his offer without seeming rude.

But then he whisked his wet jumper over his head—and she forgot to breathe, let alone look for an escape route.

'It's always freezing down here,' he said, crossing towards her. 'Even in the summer.'

She stared, her gaze riveted to his naked chest. Not just giddy any more but light-headed.

Goodness.

She'd never seen anything so beautiful. Bronzed, olive skin defined the bunch of muscle that looked so much leaner and tougher than the steroidal excess of the romance cover models she'd once fantasised about. She certainly wouldn't be fantasising about them any more.

A faded tattoo of a coiled snake writhed on his left bicep as he rubbed the garment over his hair, making it stick up in rough spikes. Her gaze locked on the springy curls of hair under his arms, which also grew much more sparsely around flat brown nipples. The dusting of hair angled down into a thin line that bisected the ridges of his six pack before disappearing beneath the low waistband of his jeans. Her heartbeat bumped against her neck as she noticed the thin white scar that stood out against the bronzed skin of his abdomen, slashing across his ribs to follow the line of his hipbone. She struggled to breathe, horrified and yet entranced by the other smaller scars she spotted marring smooth skin. She'd known he was dangerous, but she hadn't realised quite how dangerous.

Her eyes jerked to his face as he lobbed the wet sweater into a wicker laundry basket beside the washing machine. Stepping closer, he lifted the helmet out of her hands, a confident smile edging his lips. She could have sworn she could feel the heat of his skin. Or maybe that was just her body temperature going haywire, because she was about to pass out?

She drew in a lungful of air. And tasted the clean spicy scent of him.

'You cold?' he asked, dumping the helmet on a shelf. She shook her head, knowing speech was probably a bad idea.

'Come on, the apartment's a lot warmer.'

'Okay,' she mumbled, as if she needed any more heat.

Having retrieved her bag from the bike box, he hooked it over her shoulder, then guided her towards a wooden staircase that led out of the back of the garage into the rain. 'You'll need to lose the ankle-breakers,' he said, the weight of his palm on her back causing the now familiar sizzles of electricity. 'The stairs get slippery in the rain.'

She nodded, still mute, and slipped off the slingback shoes. Before she could bend to pick them up, he scooped them off the floor.

He clasped her hand and they dashed through the rain together, drops splashing on the wooden decks as they climbed to the top landing. Her breath sawed out as he led her through terrace doors into a long, narrow room with high ceilings and a marble fireplace thrown into shadow by the twilight. The starkly modern leather sofa and chairs and huge flat-screen TV contrasted with the old-world charm of the cornices on the ceiling. A light clicked on illuminating a spotlessly clean, granite and glass kitchen at the far end of the room.

'I'll get some towels,' he said, disappearing down a corridor to the right of the kitchen.

She shivered violently. The room was warm, cosy even, with the sound of the sleeting rain lashing the terrace doors, but the sight of his naked back retreating from view did nothing to stop the shaking.

Dropping her bag on the kitchen counter, she spotted her mobile in the side pocket, its message light flashing.

She read the text from Tess. *'Where r u???'*

She paused with her fingers over the key pad. What should she say? How did she explain where she was and what she was planning to do? She took in a shuddering breath.

Keep it brief. Keep it simple. And don't go into too much detail or you might chicken out.

She keyed in: *'I'm with Nick.'*

The mobile buzzed almost instantly with Tess's reply. *'OMG! U wild woman.'*

A smile quirked on Eva's lips, excitement dispelling the last of her terror. Finally, dull, swotty Eva Redmond was having a conversation like the ones she'd once overheard in the changing room before PE class or in the common room at university. The conversations she'd listened to with avid interest and secretly envied, but had never once been a part of. Because the girls she'd eavesdropped on—the pretty, confident girls who had boyfriends and a social life and didn't stress about their exams or their homework nearly as much as they did about their next date—those girls had never talked to Eva. In fact they had probably never even known she existed.

Eva tapped out: *'Don't w8 up,'* the last of her doubts lifting off her shoulders. Who knew it would feel so liberating not to be invisible any more?

Tess's reply flashed back. *'LOL. Go 4 it!'*

She shoved the phone back into the bag, next to the file folder that contained her notes on the D'Alegria case. A wayward grin spread across her face. There would be time enough for work tomorrow. Tonight, Eva Redmond was finally going to get the chance to play.

She peeled off her wet tights and buried the sodden mass in the pocket of the leather jacket. Maybe she didn't look her best, but she planned to look as presentable as possible. Clammy water dripped down under the collar as she heard the soft pad of footsteps in the hall.

Appearing out of the shadows, Nick walked towards her with predatory grace, a towel draped around his neck and his feet now as bare as his chest. The exhilaration caused by her girly text conversation peaked and Eva's teeth chattered.

Without a word, Nick took the tab of the jacket zip between his fingers. The rasp of the tiny metal teeth releasing cut through the soft patter of the slowing rain. He pushed the jacket off her shoulders, tugged it down her arms and dumped it on the sofa. Carefully locating the last of the pins in her hair, he pulled each of them out then ran his fingers through the wet curls, gently parting the tangles. The rain glistened in his damp hair as he drew the towel from around his neck, then gathered the ends of her hair and rubbed.

Eva stood trembling under his ministrations, her heartbeat rioting. A muscle in his jaw flexed while he concentrated on the task. The bodice of the dress felt like a corset closing off her air supply. Her heavy breasts swelled against the constriction as the ends of the towel fluttered over her cleavage.

Finally satisfied, he looped the towel round her neck. Holding the ends, he tugged her up onto her tiptoes. She opened her mouth on a little gasp and his tongue plundered as she placed her hands on his stomach to steady herself. The hot smooth skin tensed under her palms and her fingers touched the rough edges of the scar. As he lifted his head her breathing became so jagged she felt as if she were about to faint.

He let go of the towel, and she dropped back onto her heels. His palms cradled her elbows, his thumbs stroking the sensitive skin on the inside as his lips lifted on one side in a lopsided smile. 'I'll have to take the dress off, to dry you properly.'

The rough murmur seemed to prickle over her skin, scraping over each of the places that throbbed with need. She looked back at him, and felt the spark of impulse, the sizzle of desire and anticipation. All her life she must have had this wildness lurking inside but it had taken a man like Nick Delisantro to locate it and bring it galloping to the surface.

'I'd like that,' she heard herself murmur, her voice low and sultry and nothing like her own.

His lips quirked as he placed his hands firmly on her waist. 'You would, huh?'

She nodded.

He didn't reply, but anchored his hand on her hip and turned her to face the terrace doors. Lifting the hair draped over her shoulder, he trailed tiny kisses down her neck, sucking and nibbling and sending her senses into overdrive. The reflection of them, backlit by the kitchen light, was so erotic her knees trembled. He stood behind her, his head dark against the stark white skin of her collarbone. The zip at the back of the dress released, freeing her breasts from the too-small bodice as firm fingers eased the straps of the dress down. His eyes met hers in the rain-splattered glass as he undid the hook on her bra with a deafening click. He peeled the purple lace off leaving her naked to the waist.

His teeth fastened on the cord in her neck, feasting on the sensitive spot as his fingers traced the outline of her areolas. She raised limp arms, fastened them around his neck and arched into his hands, desperate to feel more, to have it all. She sobbed, her breath trapped in her lungs as hot callused palms cupped her breasts and caressed.

She shuddered, the pleasure so intense her knees buckled.

He swore, the harsh expletive making her eyes fly open. Grasping her waist, he spun her round to face him, then cradled her breast, and fastened his lips on the aching peak.

She held his head, the hair damp against her palms as he teased the swollen tip with his tongue, his teeth. Her thighs quivered and she moaned, scolding heat scorching down her torso to the bundle of nerves at her centre.

He raised his head, ending the devastating torment, and then shoved the dress past her hips. It settled around her ankles, leaving only the tiny swatch of lace covering her sex. She'd never felt more vulnerable, more exposed in her life, but as she saw the glazed desire in his eyes power surged.

'Put your hands round my neck,' he demanded. She obeyed, mesmerised by the hard glint of passion darkening the golden brown as he swept her up in his arms. Kicking the heavy velvet out of his way, he strode across the front room, then down the narrow corridor to the back of the apartment. Shoving open a door, he walked into a large room, its hexagonal shape marking it out as the pergola she'd admired from below.

Her breasts ached, and every inch of her skin tingled as he laid her on the large bateau bed that dominated the room. Moonlight streamed through the window, highlighting the harsh beauty of his torso. She panted, trying to calm her breathing, wipe the fog of arousal from her mind as he grabbed a foil packet out of the bedside table and flung it onto the coverlet. She clasped her arms across her swollen breasts, the heady feel of his teeth, his tongue still a visceral memory as he unsnapped his jeans, ripped open the button fly and kicked off the wet denim and cotton boxers beneath.

Her heart rammed into her throat as she got her first sight of the column of erect flesh that thrust out from the nest of hair at his groin. A shocked gasp escaped her lips as she gauged the impressive length and thickness.

Her mind engaged, and she felt a flutter of panic as the blaze of lust flooded between her thighs. She knew all about the mechanics of sex, had spent years day-dreaming about this moment. But she'd never seen a naked man in the flesh before. Let alone a naked man who was fully aroused. And she hadn't day-dreamed about anything quite that… She took a steadying breath, desire and panic twisting together in the pit of her stomach. Anything quite that enormous.

He grasped the foil packet off the bed, rolled on the latex sheath with ease and efficiency. She glanced up as he settled onto the bed beside her, dragged her easily into his arms, his erection now butting her thigh.

'Hey, what's this?' he said, sounding puzzled and amused as he took her wrists, to lift her clasped arms away from her breasts. 'Don't get shy on me, now.'

She struggled to breathe, knowing she had to relax, or this would be a thousand times more uncomfortable. Should she tell him? That this was her first time? But then he dipped his head, captured one aching peak between his teeth, and she raised off the bed, pushing her body instinctively into the exquisite torture.

Don't think. Just feel. And don't tell him, or he may stop.

As her fingers fisted on the sheet, her body bowed by the renewed onslaught of sensation, she knew that, however painful the initial penetration, she didn't want him to stop.

He explored her body with his tongue, his teeth, his lips. Suckling hard then drawing back, transferring from one breast to the other. His hand flattened against her belly. She bucked, shocked by the intensity of sensation rocketing up from her core as he cupped her, then discovered the slick burning nub. He circled and retreated, teasing her with fleeting caresses that took her to the brink but were never enough. She clung to his shoulders, sobbed out incoherent pleas for him to do more.

He gave a rough laugh. Then he touched, right at the heart of her. She opened her thighs, bumping against the knowing brush of his thumb, the nerves exploding.

She cried out, the orgasm cascading through her in strong, sure, wonderful waves.

Quivering, shaking, she kissed his cheek, laughed with delight, the rush of achievement, of abandon sensational as she floated in afterglow.

'Thank you. Thank you,' she murmured, tears of emotion, of joy sliding down her cheeks.

The sense of validation was triumphal. Sex was more wonderful, more fulfilling than her wildest fantasises, all she'd had to do was wait—for the right man to unlock the secret passion inside her.

'You're welcome.' He chuckled, sounding surprised and amused. His brows drew together as he stared down at her in the moonlight. He touched his thumb to her cheek, lifted a drop. 'That was quite a show. Do you always cry when you come?'

The inquisitive, vaguely mocking tone brought her sharply

back to reality, the hazy joy clearing to be replaced with embarrassment. Appalled at how exposed she felt—and at how much she'd let him see.

This means nothing to him.

'Not always,' she lied. She choked out what she hoped was a frivolous laugh. 'You're good at that.'

He grinned, the flash of pride almost boyish. 'Only good, huh?' he said, clasping her hips in large hands and positioning her beneath him. 'Let's see if I can do better.'

She had a moment to tense, prepare for the devastating entry and then he plunged hard.

She cried out, the pain raw and shocking, as his girth thrust through the barrier of flesh.

'What the hell?' He reared back, stopped dead, the penetration so deep she could feel every inch. 'Are you okay?'

She nodded, robbed of speech, the pain still raw, still brutal. 'Don't stop,' she said, through gritted teeth, determined to bear it.

He cradled her cheek, still lodged impossibly deep. 'Are you sure? You're so tight.'

'It'll be all right in a minute,' she said and prayed that it would be.

'Relax,' he murmured. 'You're tense.' He stroked his hand down, pressed his thumb to the punch of her pulse. He didn't move, didn't thrust. And slowly the pain receded. To be replaced by an impossible pressure. He smiled down at her, and she wondered if he somehow knew.

'Let's see if we can go for better than all right,' he said, then lifted her hips.

She sucked in a sharp, ragged breath as he settled deeper still. She gave a low groan, grateful when the pain didn't return, even though the pressure increased. His forearm strained beside her head, the muscles of his bicep bunching and releasing, as he held his weight off her. Then he drew his other hand down. Delving into the curls at her core with expert fingers, he exposed the swollen nub and flicked it with his thumb. She jerked, thrusting against him, the sudden rub of intense sensation both exquisite and shocking.

He continued to play, continued to circle and rub and flick until slowly, gradually, the swell of pleasure built again, unstoppable, unrelenting this time. The pressure then turned to a new exquisite pain as he began to move at last, rubbing some spot so deep inside, the pleasure intensified. She moaned, gripping his bicep to anchor herself and moved too, meeting the expert thrust of his hips with her own untutored movements.

She heard his harsh grunts against her ear. Felt him swell to even greater proportions, the fullness of his penis triggering a brutal, pulsing series of contractions that rolled over her. Then shattered, shooting her into oblivion.

Feeling, sensation, sanity returned in tiny incremental bits and pieces. The ragged pants of his breathing rasping in her ear, the musty scent of sex and sweat overlaying the clean fresh scent of rainwater and him, the muscled shelf of his shoulder resting on her collarbone, the large, but softening column of his erection still impaling tender flesh.

'Damn.' His low murmur cut through the silence. 'That was good.' He sounded as dazed, as disorientated as she.

He lifted off her, pulled out gently. She flinched, a groan escaping as her swollen flesh released him, the soreness a cruel reminder of the initial pain. She rolled away from him, and shifted across the bed.

As incredible as that had been, she felt fragile and wary. She'd never imagined, never realised, sex would be anything like that. The heady romances she'd read certainly hadn't prepared her for something so brutal, so basic, the elemental nature of it nothing short of animalistic.

'Hang on a minute.' One muscled forearm banded around

her waist, drawing her back into his chest. 'Where are you off to?' His lips nuzzled her neck.

'I need to…' *Get away from you,* she heard her mind shout, shocked by the renewed blast of arousal as his thumb played lazily with her nipple. She hurt, all over. She couldn't possibly want to do it again. But still the molten heat between her thighs gushed back.

She lay motionless, clamped down on the need to struggle out of his grip. She didn't want him to figure out the truth, that their coupling had been a life-altering experience for her.

She couldn't bear for him to know now that she'd been a virgin. It would make this far too intimate. And it was intimate enough already. She'd assumed this would be anonymous sex, only to discover that the intimacy of the act meant there was probably no such thing.

'I need to use the bathroom,' she said.

'All right.' His hand stroked her belly in an oddly possessive manner. 'There's an en suite over there.' His chin touched her shoulder as he nodded towards a door in the opposite wall. 'I'll keep the bed warm,' he murmured, his hand skimming down her buttocks before he released her.

The proprietary words reverberated in her head as she shot across the room naked.

She couldn't have been? Could she?

Nick frowned at the moonlight reflecting off the polished wood of the bathroom door, the niggling suspicion slowly but surely clawing its way through the sweet, heady buzz of afterglow.

Rolling over, he snapped on the bedside light, and flipped the duvet back. Then blinked several times at the two dark red splotches on the pale blue linen bed sheet.

He jerked upright, then cursed softly.

No way. Not possible.

He stared blankly for several long minutes at the evidence

before him. Then raked his hand through his hair, the contraction in his chest forcing him to finally process the truth.

Eva the sexy anthropologist was a virgin. Correction, had been a virgin. Right up until the moment he'd ploughed into her.

He swore again, a lot more forcefully this time. And pushed back the sickening wave of guilt at the memory of her face, white with shock.

How the hell was that even possible? How could a woman as alluring and spontaneous and mind-blowingly sexy as she was have waited into her twenties to have intercourse? And why had she?

A picture of her wide blue eyes, petal soft skin and the tempting sprinkle of freckles across her shoulder blades formed in his mind. He gulped down the constriction in his throat. Damn. Assuming she was in her twenties. Why hadn't he stopped long enough to ask her? To be sure?

He acknowledged the residual hum of heat in his groin, and had his answer.

Because he'd been spellbound. That was why. Even now, the memory of her lush body writhing in his arms, the weight of her full breasts in his palms and the sound of her stunned gasps as he ran his hands over the puckered pink flesh had the blood surging south. He'd been mesmerised by her ever since he'd spotted her in the gallery. And once he'd got her back here, got her naked, the last semblance of restraint had been swept away on a wave of lust so intense he'd been determined to have her.

Hearing the trickle of running water coming from behind the bathroom door, he slid out of bed and stripped off the stained bed sheet, feeling thoroughly disgusted with himself.

He'd lost control, let instinct and lust take over—something he'd worked really hard never to do again—and had sex with a woman he hadn't bothered to find out a damn thing about. He knew her name, that she had studied anthropology and that she had written a script she wanted him to look at, which had to be why she'd been so keen to meet him.

Lobbing the soiled linen into the laundry basket, he grabbed a fresh sheet out of the drawer and wrestled it on while riding out the dull flush on his cheeks.

He'd admired her honesty and her forthright manner when she'd told him their meeting hadn't been accidental. And been hopelessly turned on by her refreshingly artless approach to sex and then blinded by her quick and instinctive response to his caresses. So much so that he hadn't stopped to question her.

He let out a calming breath.

Stop beating yourself up. You're not exactly an expert on virgins.

Despite his varied and extensive experience, he'd never been any woman's first lover before. How could he have known her innocence wasn't faked? That the sheen of grateful tears in her eyes when he'd stroked her to orgasm was a sign of her inexperience and not, as he'd assumed like a conceited jerk, his superstar abilities in the sack?

He hadn't forced her. She'd been willing. More than willing. And while the possibility that she might be younger than he'd thought bothered him, surely she couldn't be a teenager. She'd been far too intellectually astute and not nearly self-absorbed enough for that.

All of which meant he was off the hook. He slung the duvet back onto the bed, but as he settled under it to wait for her return the tight feeling in his chest refused to go away.

Maybe he didn't need to feel responsible. But unfortunately he did, because while he'd had one of the most mind-blowing orgasms of his life, he'd hurt her.

His eyes narrowed, trained on the bathroom door. Which brought them to another burning question. Why hadn't she said anything? Before letting him barrel into her like that? He'd seen the shocked look on her face when he'd been putting on the condom. He was a fairly big guy, and for all her lush curves she was a small woman, but even so if she'd said something, anything, he would at least have attempted to get a stranglehold on his desire and use some degree of finesse.

A sick feeling settled in his stomach. Had she wanted him to hurt her?

The horrible suspicion that she might have been intending to use her virginity to give her some leverage tomorrow, when she showed him her script, sprang into his head. And was thankfully almost as quickly quashed. If she were that devious, wouldn't she have mentioned her virginity straight afterwards? Made a bigger deal of it? And her seduction techniques were hardly practised. Just the opposite in fact. Plus, how could she have known he would find her refreshingly untutored reaction to him such a major turn-on? Hell. He wouldn't have suspected he'd find it a turn-on himself until tonight.

He forced himself to relax back against the headboard and folded his arms over his chest, the insistent beat of his heart punctuating the seconds ticking by as he waited for her to reappear.

One thing he did know: when Miss Eva the sexy anthropologist finally ventured out of his bathroom, she was going to have a whole lot of explaining to do.

CHAPTER FIVE

CONCENTRATING on the two deep grooves bisecting her brow in the bathroom mirror, Eva forced her fingers to release their death grip on the sink.

Hiding out in Nick Delisantro's bathroom for the rest of the night is not an option.

The metallic tinkle of rain hit the fire escape outside and she shifted her attention to the partially open window. Then sighed, stifling the urge to leap onto the vanity unit, wedge herself through the small gap and run off into the night.

'Don't be ridiculous,' she whispered to her pale reflection.

Apart from the fact that she was stark naked under Nick's oversized robe, her bag was still on the kitchen counter and it was the middle of the night, she was in a strange city in a strange country and it was pouring with rain. If she didn't die of hypothermia, she'd probably get arrested. So running away was not an option either. The frown on her forehead deepened.

Plus she had an important appointment with Nick tomorrow, which she couldn't duck out of. As difficult as it was going to be to assume any kind of professional etiquette after sleeping with him, he'd probably throw her out on her ear if she showed up after doing a vanishing act in the middle of the night.

Which left option number three: be mature and dignified, something that had eluded her so far this evening, face up to her responsibilities, and give the man some kind of explanation—*before* she ran out on him.

She straightened away from the sink and glanced at the door. Assuming, of course, she ever got up the guts to stop cowering in his bathroom.

Not that she intended to tell him the truth—that her secret fantasy life had taken one wild leap into reality during the space of one motorbike ride. Not only would that be way too much information for a one-night stand, but he'd probably think she was a lunatic.

She twisted on the tap, and splashed one last dose of cold water on her cheeks. The scarlet hue making her freckles look like bullet points faded to a dusky pink.

At least she'd had one lucky break. She hadn't bled very much, so he need never know what a pathetic cliché she actually was. A twenty-four-year-old virgin, whose experience of men and sex up until fifteen minutes ago had been gleaned from the pages of romance novels.

Unfortunately she now knew the truth. That the novels had lied. Or at least been guilty of omission. They really ought to have mentioned how mortifying it was to face a complete stranger who had given you two stunning orgasms after the haze of afterglow had cleared.

Time to stop prevaricating—and face the fire. She could save the self-flagellation for tomorrow, when she was safely on the plane back to the UK, with his signed agreement to a DNA test tucked in her bag.

She yanked the lapels of the robe up to her chin and retied the belt. The sooner she faced Nick, the sooner she could start putting her night of insanity behind her. The next ten minutes were going to be awkward in the extreme. No question. And it was a pity she hadn't considered that a bit sooner. But the good news was he'd probably be just as keen to get this whole episode over with now as she was.

Her courage rallied as she gripped the door handle in a

determined fist. You never knew, he might even have fallen asleep, then she could simply leave a polite note.

Eva took two paces into the room, then stopped dead, her heartbeat and her pheromones both leaping into frantic action as her gaze landed on the bed.

With his back propped against the headboard, Nick Delisantro sat watching her.

'You're still awake.' She winced at the inane remark and the rush of blood to her nether regions. With his arms crossed over his chest, his pectoral muscles looked even more well defined than she remembered them.

Oh my. She took a steadying breath, riveted to the spot. How could she have forgotten how beautiful he was?

'Hello, Eva. Long time, no see,' he said dryly.

She felt the dusky pink rise back to scarlet. 'I'm sorry I took so long. I didn't mean to keep you awake.' She gestured down the corridor with her thumb. 'I should probably get—'

'Come here,' he said, releasing his arms and beckoned her with one finger.

She crossed to the bed as if drawn by an invisible string. It would probably be better to get this over with—her eyes dipped and then jerked back to his face—and not notice how low the duvet sat on his hips.

He patted the mattress beside him. 'Sit down.'

She perched on the edge of the bed. 'I really ought to be going,' she managed, her mouth so dry the words rasped against her throat like sandpaper. 'Tess will be wondering where I am.'

His eyes searched her face and then he lifted his hand, and brushed his thumb across her cheekbone. She stiffened, the contact unexpected. 'How old are you?' he asked gently.

'Twenty-four.'

He released a long breath. 'You look younger without make-up on,' he murmured.

'I should go,' she said more demonstrably this time, the insistent melting sensation between her legs getting more acute.

She tried to stand, but he grasped her wrist, and held on. 'I don't think so.'

'Why not?' she asked breathlessly, the feel of his thumb absently caressing the thin skin of her wrist not doing a thing for her sanity issues.

'Why didn't you tell me?'

'Tell you what?' she asked, the blood surging into her cheeks as her stomach dipped. Did he know? How could he know?

'That this was your first time?'

She swallowed convulsively, looked away from his seeking gaze, the blood coursing so hard now she was fairly sure her cheeks could double as fog lamps. 'I don't know what you're talking about…' Her voice trailed off as she faced him. She'd never been a good liar, and from his penetrating stare it was clear he wasn't fooled.

'I had to change the sheets,' he said matter-of-factly, and her cheeks burst into flame.

She stared down at her hands, clasped in her lap, and his long fingers still looped around her wrist. Could he feel her pulse hitting his thumb like a jack-hammer?

She croaked out a laugh. Forget about awkward, this was now officially the most humiliating experience of her entire life. And given her pitiful history with members of the opposite sex that was quite an achievement.

Hooking a finger under her chin, he raised her gaze to his. 'Why didn't you say something?'

Good question.

And one she had no intention of answering in any detail. 'I thought…' She paused, gave a stiff shrug. 'I thought you might stop if you knew.'

His thumb continued to circle her pulse point in lazy strokes. 'Why would I have stopped?'

'I don't know...' she murmured. 'I thought you might not want the responsibility... Or something.'

He sent her a puzzled smile. 'You're an educated woman who's past the age of consent. Why would your virginity be my responsibility?'

The blush flared back to life. 'It's not. Obviously it's not,' she said, backtracking furiously to cover the excruciating embarrassment. 'That's not what I meant.'

He tipped his head to one side, considering. 'So what did you mean?'

How had she dug herself into such a huge hole? And how was she going to climb out again with even a small measure of her dignity in tact? 'Just that, if you knew I didn't have a clue what I was doing, you might not want to...' She mumbled, the last of her confidence leaking away under his unwavering gaze. 'You know... Do it... With me.'

Her pride crumbled to dust when he choked out an incredulous laugh. 'You're not serious?'

The astonished amusement in his tone crucified her. He was laughing at her, and while she already knew how ridiculous she was, she couldn't see the funny side. 'I have to go,' she said, tugging on her hand.

Instead of letting go, his fingers tightened. 'Shh, calm down, sweetheart.'

The careless endearment touched that lonely place deep inside her she'd always tried so hard to ignore and her abject humiliation was complete. She'd always known she was a pathetic cliché, but she'd never known quite how pathetic.

She pulled back, wanting not just to run away now but to hide under a very large rock.

He gripped her other wrist and drew her back towards him. Still chuckling, he pressed his forehead to hers. Then to her astonishment placed a kiss on her temple.

'Eva, you're one of the sweetest, cutest, sexiest women I've ever met. How could you not know that?'

He gave his head a little shake, the stunned pleasure the compliment caused making her chest hurt.

'Really?' she asked, then flushed redder, realising how needy she sounded.

But he didn't seem to notice, the mocking twist of his lips disappearing as he smiled.

'Put it this way, I nearly lost it in the living room and I hadn't even got you naked.' His voice had roughened, scraping over her skin. 'Are you in any pain?' he asked softly.

She shook her head. 'It's a bit tender, that's all,' she said, her senses reeling as the swell of emotion thickened her throat. She swallowed, forced the boulder back down. He couldn't possibly know how much it meant to her to know the passion between them had been mutual.

Giving a gentle tug on the tie of her robe, his hand snuck under the towelling and settled on the curve of her waist. 'Come to bed.'

The husky invitation sent all sorts of fireworks off in her nerve-endings, but she caught his wrist, stopped his hand from wandering. 'I don't think I can do it again yet.'

He grinned. 'I meant, so we can get some sleep.' Taking his hand out of her robe, he rubbed his thumb under her eye. 'You look shattered. And for that I am responsible.'

She opened her mouth to try and deny it, but it stretched into an enormous yawn.

He laughed. 'I rest my case.' He lifted the duvet and scooted back to make a space for her. 'I won't ravish you again tonight. You have my word.'

Given the smouldering look in his eyes, she wasn't sure she could trust him. But the sight of his muscular body, shadowed by the duvet, was so tempting, and the thought of spending a little more time in his arms, however meaningless, so seductive, she nodded.

He'd been patient and understanding and surprisingly gallant. And he'd told her she was the sexiest woman he'd ever met. Which was obviously a lie, but a really nice one.

She settled into the lee of his body, curled her back into his chest. He anchored one arm around her waist, bundling her into the towelling robe like a child, and kissed the back of her head. 'Sleep tight.'

The feel of his big body cocooned around hers felt so safe, so comforting she drew in a deep breath, let out a shaky sigh. Her wild night hadn't been a complete catastrophe after all.

While the whole experience had been a lot more affecting than she would have anticipated. Not to mention exhausting. She'd remember Nick Delisantro—and the rainy autumn night in San Francisco she lost her virginity—for the rest of her life.

She closed her eyes, the lids weighing several tons, and drifted into a sleep filled with wonderfully vivid and earthily erotic dreams.

Nick watched the rain run in rivulets down the bedroom's bay window, the droplets tinged orange in the dawn light, and diligently counted the streams. Eva shifted beside him, her flannel-clad bottom bumping his hip. He sucked in a breath, heat surging back to his groin, her scent flooding his senses— and he lost count of the rivulets. Again.

What had possessed him to suggest she stay the night? He wasn't a snuggler, and he wasn't responsible for Eva despite the dark smudges under her eyes or the astonished wonder on her face when he'd told her how sexy she was.

But even knowing that, he'd been lying here for hours now, kept awake by the double whammy of an erection that shot back to attention every time she brushed against him and the questions that refused to stop bouncing around in his head like hyperactive sheep.

How had a woman as passionate as Eva stayed a virgin for so long? And why had she? And why the hell had she picked him, of all people, to be her first? A guy who'd left innocent behind a lifetime ago.

Easing his arm out from under her shoulders, he rolled away from her onto his side.

The answers didn't concern him. They didn't matter. He shouldn't even be asking the questions. Just as he'd told her—and she'd agreed—those were her choices, not his. But somehow, he couldn't stop the questions from circling like buzzards, and pecking away at his certainty.

He stared at the early morning light shining on the ugly antique dresser he'd inherited when he bought the apartment two years ago. He should wake her up. Call her a cab. He had to be up in a couple of hours, had to get the first draft of the script he was working on finished this week if he was going to meet the production deadline. But somehow he hadn't been able to find the will to do it while her soft, scented body was curled so trustingly by his side.

For some strange, inexplicable reason, he'd wanted to keep her with him. For tonight.

He shut his eyes, felt the tired, gritty texture on the lids that signalled insomnia. Willing himself to ignore the murmur of her breathing and the aroma of spring flowers and talcum powder that teased his nostrils, his brain finally began to unwind, and the erection to soften.

As he fell into a fitful sleep he promised himself he would hustle her out first thing in the morning no matter how soft and tempting she looked in his bed. This was physical attraction. Pure and simple. All he had to do was control it, the way he'd been doing for years.

And he wasn't going to ask a single one of those damn questions either.

Those were her choices. Her business. And nothing whatsoever to do with him.

CHAPTER SIX

NICK rolled his shoulders to ease out the kinks, and tried to persuade himself the freezing shower had refreshed him. Grabbing a pair of old sweatpants and a UCLA T-shirt out of the dresser, he slipped them on, his eyes fixed on the woman still curled on his bed.

He felt the familiar tightening in his groin. The sunlight streaming through the window gave her pale skin a soft glow and cast a halo of light over the curls of hair mussed around her cheek. She looked cuter than a Botticelli angel. His gaze dipped to the sliver of cleavage visible above the lapels of the robe she'd slept in. An exceptionally sexy Botticelli angel.

He pushed the drawer shut, a little too heavily, and steeled himself against the tinge of guilt when her eyes fluttered open.

It was nearly eleven. He needed to get going. He had a lot to do today. Especially if he was going to meet her for that appointment he'd promised. Which, now he thought about it, he wished he hadn't. Seeing her again probably wasn't the smartest idea.

She scrambled upright, her dazed expression finally focusing on him. The robe fell off one shoulder and she clutched the lapels together, covering herself too late to stop the shot of arousal hitting his crotch. He shoved his hands into the pockets of the sweatpants.

She pushed the hair out of her face with an unsteady hand. 'I—I'm sorry, I overslept,' she stammered, her voice smoky with sleep. 'I should…' She glanced around, disorientated. 'I should get going.'

The apologetic tone kicked off his temper—which wasn't in the best of conditions anyway. He'd had a total of four hours' sleep and his body still seemed to have a mind of its own, despite the ice-cold shower he'd treated it to. 'Stop apologising.'

'I'm sorry?'

He propped his butt against the dresser, braced his hands against the surface as he studied her. 'You just did it again.'

'Did what?' she asked, chewing on her full bottom lip, and making him want to chew on it too.

'Said sorry.'

'Oh, yes, I see. I'm sor—' She stopped.

'See what I mean,' he said sharply, irritated by the flicker of vulnerability and confusion in her eyes. 'Why do you keep apologising?'

'I've outstayed my welcome,' she said at last, which was hardly an answer. She lifted the duvet and he got a good look at her slim calves as she put her bare feet on the floor, reminding him how naked she was under his robe. 'I'll get my clothes, then get out of your way.'

'They're over there.' He nodded towards the window seat in the bay.

He'd headed straight to the kitchen after waking up, to gulp down a gallon of water—but his throat had dried right up again when he'd spotted her clothing, draped across the living area. It had been hard as hell not to fantasise about taking the skimpy bit of lace and the heavy velvet gown off her as he'd gathered them off the floor and dumped them in the bedroom.

Hence the freezing shower.

'Thank you.' She crossed the room to the bay. 'Do you mind if I use your bathroom? I promise not to hog it this time.'

As she bent to pick up the clothes the robe gaped, and he spotted her nipple, before she covered it hastily.

'Sure,' he murmured, determined not to ask the question making his head hurt or give in to the desire to tug the robe off, and make the ripe peak harden against his tongue.

But then she walked past him and his hand shot out to grasp her forearm as the fresh sultry scent of her filled his nostrils. 'Why me?' he demanded.

She jerked to a halt, her violet eyes huge. 'Sorry?'

'Stop apolo—' He cut off the surly command, seeing her flinch. 'What made you pick me?'

Her long lashes hit her cheeks as her gaze dropped away, but she didn't answer.

'To be your first?' he prompted, although he was pretty sure from the nuclear blush fanning out across her chest and spreading up her throat she had understood the question.

'I don't…' She hesitated, her chin still tucked against her chest. 'When you looked at me that first time, it made me feel…' She addressed her toes, the words trailing into silence.

It made her feel *what?* But then he recalled how she had writhed in his arms when he'd undressed her, and figured he knew.

Her chin lifted. 'I think, possibly, on an entirely subconscious level, when I researched you, I must have decided you would be a good choice. Because you're so assured, sexually. And I'm not.'

When I researched you.

He released her. Okay, that was intrusive.

'Right.' He dug his fists back into his pockets, trying to muster the required anger at what she'd revealed. Because if he'd understood her right—and, given his sleep deprivation and the fact that all of his blood had drained out of his head, that was debatable—she'd just told him she'd dug into his private life so she could engineer a meeting with him. But she sounded so earnest and sincere, those Bambi eyes were doing funny things to his equilibrium.

'I need coffee.' He scrubbed his hands down his face. 'I'll call you a cab while you're in the shower,' he grunted, not as enthusiastic as he should have been at the thought of getting rid of her.

'A cab would be great, thank you,' she said, before she hurried away with her clothes.

He frowned as he headed for the kitchen. He rarely did sleepovers, because he preferred not to deal with the morning after. And the demands on his time that inevitably followed.

The fact that Eva Redmond hadn't made a single demand—hadn't even seemed surprised when he'd offered to call a cab—should have pleased him. It didn't.

He'd made a rash decision, and led with his lust instead of his common sense last night. So why was he so tempted to make another one this morning?

He emptied the coffee pot, started going through the ritual of brewing a fresh pot. Time to mainline caffeine, before he lost his mind completely and invited her to stay for breakfast... So he could bombard her with all the questions that had kept him awake most of the night. And then sweet-talk her back into bed.

Nick inhaled the first precious sip of scalding black coffee and tried to ignore the buzz of the mobile phone coming from Eva's bag. He glanced down the corridor to the bedroom door.

Where the hell was she? He wanted her gone before the last of his will power seeped into his pants. The ringing cut off, then started right back up again.

He slapped the mug down and grabbed the bag. After rummaging for a few seconds trying to locate the phone, he dumped the contents onto the countertop. An array of female paraphernalia poured out: pens, a make-up case, a roll of antacids, a notebook, a sheath of papers, tissues, a cotton sweater. Finally he spotted the buzzing mobile under a file folder.

Swiping it up, he clicked the answer button. 'What?' he barked into the receiver.

There was a slight pause, then a succinct female voice asked, 'Oh, hello. Is that Niccolo Delisantro?'

'The name's Nick,' he corrected, but softened his tone, the woman's precise English accent reminding him of Eva. 'I take it you're the busybody friend,' he added, vaguely recalling the long, skinny girl in the blue dress from the previous evening.

The woman laughed. 'Correct. And being a busybody, I'm busy trying to find out where Eva is.'

Leaning back against the countertop, he lifted his coffee mug to his lips, took another satisfying sip. 'She's in my shower,' he said, the odd feeling of satisfaction coming from nowhere.

'I see.' The woman didn't sound particularly surprised at the revelation. 'Is she spending the day with you, then?' she asked.

His heart bumped. 'No,' he said, too quickly. 'She's leaving once she's dressed.'

There was a longer pause, then the woman came back on the line. 'Could you ask her to give Tess a call?'

'Sure.'

'Excellent. Thanks. It's been nice talking to you,' she said crisply.

'Yeah.' He clicked the phone off, dumped it back on the countertop. And glared at it. What was with the heart bump? He didn't want to spend the day with Eva. Didn't want to know her secrets. The sooner she left, the better.

He contemplated the bedroom door again as he sipped the coffee, not even sure he could convince himself. What was it about her that made her different from all the other women he'd slept with? It had to be the whole virginity business. Somehow he'd got hung up on it. Crossing to the coffee maker, he refilled his cup.

Snap out of it, Delisantro. You're not thinking straight.

This ended here. Now. No more questions. And no more answers. It would only make her more of a distraction.

He stared at the debris sprawled across the counter, briefly contemplated looking through her stuff. But then dismissed the thought. He ought to stick her things back in her bag. Snooping would imply a level of interest in her he didn't have.

Picking up the file folder, he started to shove it back in her bag, when he spotted the words typed neatly on the label stuck across the top: Delisantro/De Rossi.

He lowered the mug, his heart beating right into his throat.

What the…? Why did she have a file on him? And who was De Rossi?

He flicked up the flap and peered inside, not caring any more about her privacy. Stapled to the top of a sheath of typed pages was an old press clipping. He recognised the grainy black and white photo at the centre of the layout instantly, even though he hadn't seen it in more than twenty years.

Coffee sloshed over the rim of his mug as his heart punched his larynx. He placed the mug on the countertop.

The innocuous headline: 'Family-Run Trattoria Brings Taste of Tuscany to Tufnell Park' blurred as he stared at the picture of his family below it—or, rather, the people he'd thought were his family—standing outside the tiny Italian restaurant in North London where he'd grown up.

There was his little sister Ruby, eight years old and already stunningly beautiful, showing off her best Sunday Mass dress while grinning precociously at the camera. He stood to her right, looking lanky and uncomfortable as he tugged at the starched collar and tie threatening to throttle him. And on Ruby's left stood Carmine Delisantro, with the ready smile spread across his robust features Nick would always remember. A band of emotion tightened around his heart as he blinked, noticing that Carmine's mane of hair was already thinning in his early thirties, and his head had been level with Nick's. How could they have been the same height? He'd only been twelve when the photo had been snapped by a local journalist doing an article on the family restaurant. Always in his memory Carmine had seemed like a lion of a man, his warm, vocal presence so much larger than life.

Dad.

The word echoed in his head as his thumb touched the faded newsprint. The band squeezed painfully, but just as the guilt and regret threatened to choke him his gaze settled on the woman standing on Carmine's other side in the far left of the picture, with her arm looped around her husband's waist and her head tucked on his shoulder. Nick studied her striking face, her statuesque figure, the lush lips, the glorious waves of hair, so like his own, and those dark sultry laughing eyes that had held so many cruel secrets.

Confusion and anguish washed over him, until the tide of grief turned into a wave of resentment.

Isabella Delisantro. His mother.

Eva paused at the entrance to the living room, not sure what to make of the scene before her. Nick stood with his back to her, his head bent. But why was her stuff strewn across the kitchen counter? Had he been going through her things? She tried to feel affronted, but all she could manage was dismay.

However much she might have researched about him in the last fortnight, and however intimate they had been last night. She didn't know him. And she knew even less about what to do in this situation.

Why had he been so surly when she'd woken up? Was he just not much of a morning person? Or had she done something wrong? Something she was unaware of? Was he entitled to look through her stuff, because they'd slept together? Did it give him certain rights she didn't know about? Because she'd never been in a relationship with anyone before, she didn't know if the normal rules of privacy still applied.

She was completely clueless about morning-after etiquette. She crossed her arms over her chest, desperately self-conscious about the plunging neckline of the velvet gown, and her total lack of relationship knowledge.

'Um… Hi,' she murmured, talking to Nick's rigid back. 'Did my bag explode?'

He spun round, the hard glint in his eyes making her take an involuntary step back.

'What's this?' The frigid tone of voice matched the glacial expression on his face. He held up the papers in his hand, and she recognised the contents from the De Rossi file.

'Those are my research notes,' she replied as the shiver of apprehension shimmered up her spine. If he'd seemed surly in the bedroom, he seemed coldly furious now.

'Your *research* notes?' His voice rose to a shout as he emphasised the angry words by slapping the papers down on the counter. She flinched, shocked by the barely suppressed violence in the gesture.

He braced his palms on the countertop. 'Who the hell are you? And who's De Rossi?'

She tensed. 'I'm Eva Redmond. I work for Roots Registry.' She cleared her throat, ashamed at the quiver in her voice. 'I…I thought you knew. Vincenzo De Rossi, the Duca D'Alegria is our client. I emailed your agent, countless times.' She'd only given minimal details, had intended to tell Nick the whole story face-to-face, but even so she'd assumed he knew who she was. Why she had wanted the appointment.

'I don't know any Duca D'Alegria.'

'He's an Italian duke, the last in the direct line of the house of De Rossi in the province of Alegria.' She tightened her arms, trying not to be put off by the sharp frown on his face. 'The duca's main residence is the Alegria Palazzo on the banks of Lake Garda,' she babbled on. She should have clarified the situation last night, before she'd got onto his bike. Why hadn't she? Heat pulsed in her cheeks, swiftly followed by guilt. She knew why. And it had had nothing to do with her job. 'The family owns sixty-thousand acres, a thriving olive pressing business, two vineyards and several properties in the Tuscan—'

'Stop right there!' He held up his hand to emphasise the point. 'What the hell has any of this got to do with me?'

'He's your...' She paused, her tongue going numb. He looked so angry. Resentment was rolling off him in waves. She couldn't tell him the rest. Not like this. Not after what they'd done together. Maybe it hadn't meant much to him, but it meant something to her. And however little she knew about him, she didn't want to hurt him.

He slapped his hand on the counter. 'He's my *what?*'

'We have reason to believe...' She swallowed, the sick feeling in her stomach surging up her throat. 'We have reason to believe his son, Conte Leonardo Vittorio Vincenzo De Rossi, may have been your biological father.' But the truth was there was no maybe about it. Having met the duca, and seen photos of his son, as soon as she'd got a good look at Nick Delisantro she hadn't had a single doubt about his ancestry. 'Which would make the duca your grandfather,' she continued. 'And you his only direct descendant.'

She let out a breath, her throat aching at the thought of what might be going through his mind. About the man he had believed to be his biological father. The man he'd spent the first sixteen years of his life with.

'I'm so sorry. I realise this news must come as a shock.'

But he didn't look shocked, she realised as his gaze bored into hers. In fact, he was displaying none of the reactions she had prepared herself for—shock, disbelief, confusion or, worse, hurt. Temper flashed once more in his eyes, and then his gaze raked over her. And all she saw was disgust.

'So that's his name. Leonardo De Rossi. Thanks,' he said,

contempt dripping from every syllable. 'I've always wondered who my mother screwed.'

Eva drew in a shaky breath. Not sure she'd heard him right. But how could she mistake the bitterness in his tone, or the look of derision now levelled at her?

'And you're on some kind of commission,' he asked, but it didn't sound like a question, 'to locate me, right?'

She shook her head. 'I receive a salary, but the company does get a commission from our client, once he's satisfied that you're the baby mentioned in his son's journal. Leonardo wrote a...'

He flipped up a palm and she stopped in mid-sentence, the explanation dying on her lips. 'Spare me the details. I'm not interested in the duca, or his son.' He folded his arms over his chest, propped his butt against the countertop. 'But I am interested in you.' He flicked his gaze back over her figure. 'You're quite the little operator, aren't you? I've got to admit, the virginity was a nice touch. It threw me off for a while.' He huffed out a contemptuous laugh. 'What were you doing? Saving it up for the perfect mark?'

The lump of emotion swelled in her throat as the heat soared into her cheeks. He couldn't mean what she thought he meant? That wasn't possible. This wasn't the man who had held her last night, whose arms she had slept in. Who had treated her with a care and consideration she knew now she probably hadn't deserved. She opened her mouth, to explain. Then closed it again. He was looking at her as if she were scum. Worse than scum.

'I don't...' She pushed the words out, nerves and guilt and horror writhing in her stomach like venomous snakes. 'I don't know what you're trying to imply.'

'Really?' He laughed again, the harsh sound echoing against the room's hard surfaces. He strolled easily round the counter. She stepped back as he approached, rubbed her hands over her upper arms, the heat of his temper searing her skin.

'You can stop the innocent act now. I'm wise to it.'

'I don't understand.'

He cupped her cheek, his rough palm cool against her burning skin. 'Damn, but you're good.'

'I'm not…' The denial caught in her throat. 'Whatever you're thinking, it isn't true.'

He wrapped his arm round her waist, jerked her against him. 'You know what's ironic?' he murmured as his scent filled her senses, the outline of his arousal shocking her almost as much as the melting response at her core.

She pressed her palms against his chest, tried to push away from him, but he only tugged her closer, buried his head against her neck.

'You played your ace for nothing,' he whispered against her ear, his lips brushing the pulse point hammering her throat.

She braced her arms, horrified by the sizzle of response shimmering down to her core, the moisture flooding from her thighs. The man thought she was some kind of con artist. How could she still be so susceptible to him?

He nipped at her ear lobe. 'What a shame you didn't do a better job with your research. If you had you'd know I'm not the noble type.' His hand cupped her breast. And she gasped, the nipple puckering through the velvet as he rubbed his thumb across the tip. He chuckled, the sound hollow and smug. 'You were saving it up for nothing, sweetheart. But let's not let it go to waste. Right?'

'Please don't do this.' The tears stinging her eyes only added to her humiliation. She bit into her lip, desperate to get out, to get away, before he saw her cry.

He lifted his head at the blare of a car horn from outside. 'Well, what do you know? Saved by your cab bell.'

He let her go, and she scrambled back.

'Go on, get lost,' he said, the mocking twist of his lips brutal in its contempt. He swept a hand towards her stuff. 'And take your *research* with you.'

She lifted her bag from the counter, shoved the contents back into it, her hands shaking but her back ramrod straight. The tears scoured her throat as she gulped them back.

You have to hold it together, long enough to get out of here.

She slung the bag over her shoulder, made herself face him. 'I'm sorry. I thought you knew who I was. I didn't mean for any of this to happen,' she said, politeness the only shield she had.

'Then I guess we're both sorry. Aren't we?' he said, his voice as flat and expressionless as his eyes.

Somehow even his anger was better than his contempt. She rushed through the terrace doors. Her bare feet slapped against the wooden decking as she fled, not just from him, but from her own stupidity and inadequacy.

She clenched her teeth, pressed the heel of her palm against her breastbone as the cab whisked away from the kerb. The pain and confusion felt fresh and raw and jagged as the romance of her one wild night shattered inside her like the fragile illusion it was.

How could she ever have believed, even for one night, that she could be anything other than what she was? A cowardly academic who'd spent her whole life day-dreaming about being reckless and adventurous and then doing exactly what she was told.

CHAPTER SEVEN

'WHAT is going on, Eva? Bob informs me he finally got a reply from Delisantro's agent and the guy told him Delisantro not only wants nothing to do with this company, but he specifically doesn't want anything to do with you.'

'I'm so sorry, Mr Crenshawe.' Eva gripped the polyester weave of the seat cushion and hunched into the seat, the pain as fresh and raw as it had been a week ago. Sweat pooled under the armpits of her tailored suit. 'I had hoped Mr Delisantro would be more willing to cooperate with Bob,' she mumbled, the jagged little shards of agony piercing her chest at this renewed evidence of Nick's contempt.

Hadn't she suffered enough for her foolishly reckless and fanciful behaviour a week ago?

She'd confessed to her boss, Henry Crenshawe, that her trip had been a failure as soon as she'd got back from San Francisco. Mr Crenshawe had subjected her to a ten-minute lecture on her appalling lack of people skills, and then taken her off the account, which she'd been pathetically grateful for. She didn't want to have to contact Nick again.

But she'd been far too humiliated by her gross lack of judgement and professionalism—not to mention the presence of those jagged little shards that came back every time she thought of Nick—to admit the whole truth to her boss or anyone else. That she'd got carried away by some ridiculous flight of fancy and the nuclear blip to her usually tame libido as soon as she'd set eyes on Nick Delisantro—and lost sight of everything that was important in her life in the space of one night. Her responsibilities to Roots Registry and to her job hadn't even entered her head. And for that she felt not just guilty and embarrassed but so angry with herself she wanted to scream. She'd put a job she adored in jeopardy. But what upset her more was the knowledge that Nick's contempt still hurt so much, a week after he'd kicked her out of his apartment.

How foolish was she to have believed that he might have reconsidered? And decided that she wasn't such a terrible person after all? And why should it even matter? She was never going to see him again.

'Yeah, well he isn't cooperating.' The irritation on Henry Crenshawe's face made it quite clear she wasn't going to be given any slack. 'What exactly is it that Delisantro has against you? Because if we knew that, we might be able to fix it. Get back in his good graces. The company needs this commission—it's prestigious as hell. The publicity is priceless. Alegria has three other heir-hunting companies that I know of looking for his heir. And we've got the jump on them. Because we've already located the guy.' Crenshawe yanked at his collar, his pudgy face going a mottled red. Eva's heart, the jagged little shards still prickling, sank to her toes.

She would have to tell her boss the truth. 'It's a private issue, between myself and Mr Delisantro,' she mumbled, desperate to stave off the inevitable.

'Private how?' Crenshawe demanded. 'You were only in San Francisco for one night. I know your people skills are non-existent,' he said, his voice rising. 'But even you couldn't have annoyed him that much in one night.'

She could hear the incredulity in Crenshawe's voice, and knew what he was thinking. How could his quiet, timid and inconspicuous researcher even have been noticed by a man as dynamic as Nick Delisantro, let alone have made enough of an impression on him to annoy him to this extent?

The realisation triggered something inside her—and the jagged little shards of misery were obliterated by a surge of anger.

Eva straightened in her chair, and her gaze lifted to the man who had always regarded her with benign contempt. Mr Crenshawe wouldn't expect Nick Delisantro to notice her, because like most of the people she knew, he had never really noticed her either. Henry Crenshawe had always taken her work completely for granted, had never given her the credit she was due.

Roots Registry hadn't located the Duca D'Alegria's missing heir, *she* had—after weeks of painstaking research on the historical data, most of which had had to be translated from Italian. It had been a mammoth task, checking marriage records, tracing the movements of every young bride within a fifty-mile radius of the Alegria estate in the year in question and then correlating the birth certificates of the babies born to them.

And it wasn't the first time her concentrated and creative investigation of the known facts and her diligent attention to detail had pulled in a major account. Even so, she'd been the only one of Crenshawe's researchers not to be considered for a promotion when the company had expanded a year ago. She was paid less than all her male colleagues and she'd only had one modest bonus in three years. While she adored the job she did at Roots Registry, she'd always shied away from any contact with her boss, because she knew he was a sexist blowhard who didn't understand or appreciate the work she did… Except when it came to the bottom line.

What made her temper spike, though, was the fact that Crenshawe's scorn towards her and her efforts had been partly her own fault, because she'd never once stood up for herself.

Until now.

Yes, she'd made a mistake sleeping with Nick Delisantro. But his negative reaction to the news of his grandfather's existence had not been caused by their night together. He'd clearly already been aware of his illegitimacy before she'd said anything. And the deep-seated resentment there had nothing whatsoever to do with her.

But more than that, Crenshawe was wrong about her. She wasn't the mouse he clearly thought she was. Not any more.

Nick Delisantro *had* noticed her. She hadn't been invisible to Nick. And while it might have been better for her employment prospects if she hadn't had sex with him, she was through feeling guilty or ashamed about what she'd done. She didn't deserve Henry Crenshawe's contempt, any more than she deserved Nick Delisantro's.

'I slept with Nick Delisantro that night,' she announced, pleased with the firm tone and her refusal to relinquish eye contact when Crenshawe's eyebrows shot up to his receding hairline. 'And he misconstrued my motives the following morning.'

'You did *what?*' Crenshawe yelped, the sheen of sweat on his forehead glistening. 'You… You…' His double chin wobbled with fury, the mottled colour in his cheeks turning scarlet. 'You stupid little tart.'

He was going to fire her. She could see it in the vindictive light that came into his beady eyes as he stomped around the office, gesticulating wildly and throwing out a series of increasingly personal insults about her and her work.

Her fingers released on the seat cushion and she kept her chin thrust out, more than ready to take the blow, an odd sense of calm and detachment settling over her.

Well, what d'you know? Mr Crenshawe has noticed me at last.

* * *

Nick tapped the parting line of dialogue into the template on his computer. Then paused to reread the scene he'd spent all morning sweating blood over. And groaned.

His detective hero sounded like someone with a borderline personality disorder. He ran his fingers through his hair, then stabbed the mouse to close the script window on the laptop.

Getting up from the desk, he crossed to the window, glared down at the street below which was all but deserted in the middle of the afternoon on a workday. Maybe if he got out of the apartment for a few hours, took a ride on his bike and blew the cobwebs out of his head. But as soon as the thought registered he dismissed it.

The bike was out. He'd gone for a ride yesterday, and somehow ended up on the Marin Headland, the memory of Eva Redmond's lush body plastered against his back and the high-pitched whoop of her laughter as they'd crossed the bridge reverberating through his subconscious every inch of the way.

Why couldn't he get her out of his head? It had been a full week since that night. The woman was an operator, had investigated him and his origins and then had the gall to sleep with him without telling him the truth about who she was. That should have been more than enough to end his fascination.

He swore softly, slung a hand into the pocket of the sweatpants he wore when writing. How had she got her hooks into him so deep?

He squinted against the afternoon sun shining through the study window and pictured her face the last time he'd seen it. The pallor of her skin, her lips trembling and those wide translucent blue eyes, the pupils dilated with shock.

Instead of the resentment, the cleansing anger that had sustained him for the last seven days, he finally acknowledged the trickle of guilt.

'Hell!' The expletive cut the quiet like a knife.

Eva Redmond might not have been one hundred per cent

forthcoming about who she was, but there was no getting around the fact that he had seduced her. Not the other way around.

As soon as he'd spotted her in the Union Square gallery, her glorious curves displayed to perfection in red velvet, her shy but direct gaze locked with his, he'd wanted her. And while he'd become a lot more cautious in the last decade or so, a lot more discerning about who he pursued, one thing hadn't changed. When he saw a woman he wanted, he went after her.

The only difference with Eva was that he had been more relentless, more eager and more determined in his pursuit. There had been numerous signs of how innocent, how out-of-her-depth she was, long before he'd taken her virginity, and he'd chosen to ignore every one of them to have her. So whose fault was it really that he'd ended up getting burned? Plus when he replayed all the conversations they'd had during their evening together—something he'd done with alarming regularity in the last seven days—he could see she'd tried to tell him who she was. And he'd stopped her elaborating, because he hadn't wanted to hear anything that might stop him getting her into bed.

He braced his hand on the window sill, forced himself to confront the truth. He'd done a lot of crummy things in his life. None of which he was proud of. But some of them had been necessary to survive. When you ran away from home at sixteen with just the clothes on your back and a belly full of anger, you ended up doing a lot of things that you would later regret. And he'd done more than his fair share.

He was enough of a pragmatist, though, to realise that he couldn't go back and undo those things now. And in many ways, he wouldn't want to. He wasn't a hypocrite and he knew that what he'd managed to make of his life had been largely due to that feral survival instinct—and the burning anger that had kept him strong and resilient in the face of often impossible odds. You couldn't go back, you had to go forward. But that didn't mean he could keep repeating those mistakes over and over again.

The only way he was going to be able to put this episode behind him was to see Eva Redmond again—and wipe that vision of her eyes bright with unshed tears out of his head.

Unfortunately, seeing Eva had the potential to open up a whole other can of worms.

He huffed out a harsh laugh, felt the hum of heat pulse through his system as he recalled the sight of Eva reflected in the glass, her nipples large and distended, and her soft sighs of pleasure spurring him on. He'd woken in a hot sweat every night since that night. His sex hard and erect, and throbbing with the urge to bury himself deep inside the tight clasp of her body. He'd got so damn wound up by the erotic memories he hadn't been sleeping properly, had barely been able to write—and everything he had written was terrible.

So the urge to see Eva again wasn't entirely altruistic. Given the shoddy way he'd treated her the morning after, he doubted she was going to be all that amenable to jumping back into bed with him—but that didn't seem to bother his libido.

The bright trill of his phone had him jerking upright. He turned to stare at it flashing on his desk. Probably his agent Jim wanting to know how the script was going. Not a conversation he really wanted to be having, seeing as the damn thing was going nowhere fast. But even so, he picked up the handset. Better to be lying to Jim than wrestling pointlessly with the apparently insolvable problem of Eva Redmond.

'Hi,' he said, struggling to inject some enthusiasm into the greeting.

'Hello, may I speak to Niccolo Delisantro?' replied a male voice with crisp and efficient British diction.

'Speaking, although the name's Nick,' he corrected, curious even though he didn't want to be. The only people who had called him Niccolo in recent memory were Eva and her friend Tess.

'I'm terribly sorry, Mr Delisantro. Nick,' came the effusive and fawning reply.

'Who is this?' Nick said, feeling less curious and more annoyed by the second.

'My name is Henry Crenshawe, I'm the managing director of Roots Registry. We're based in the UK. We do genealogical research for high-profile clients who wish to discover the—'

'Cut to the chase, Henry,' Nick interrupted the flow of unnecessary information as the short hairs on the back of his neck tingled. Roots Registry? Wasn't that the name of Eva's employer?

He heard a slight pause on the other end of the line, then Crenshawe's voice came back, the tone oily and obsequious. 'This is a very delicate situation, Mr Delisantro. I'm calling to offer my sincere apologies for the reprehensible conduct of our former employee Miss Eva Redmond. I can't stress enough our absolute—'

'What do you mean your *former* employee?' Nick asked as his heartbeat kicked up a notch.

'We fired her, of course,' the man replied, in an officious voice, and the trickle of guilt turned into a torrent.

'As soon as we discovered her grossly inappropriate behaviour during her visit to San Francisco,' Crenshawe continued in the same pompous tone. But Nick couldn't really hear what the guy was pontificating about.

Eva had lost her job over their night together.

'And I'd like to assure you she will never get another job in the genealogical research industry again after this incident—'

'Wait a minute,' Nick cut in, his temper finally putting in an appearance. 'How did you find out we slept together?' Was he being watched by these people?

He thought he heard a slight choking sound, then a supercilious little laugh. 'Um, well, Miss Redmond admitted to the indiscretion, Mr Delisantro, this afternoon.'

He raked his fingers through his hair.

Damn it, why had she told them? But even as he asked himself the question he could see the guilty flush on her cheeks when she'd admitted to being a virgin—as if she'd tricked him or something—and he knew the answer. Because she was an honest and forthright and hopelessly trusting person. Unlike him.

And to think he'd accused her of being an operator. What a joke. Eva Redmond was about as devious as Snow White.

'Here at Roots Registry we couldn't possibly condone that kind of behaviour,' Crenshawe continued with the same self-righteous indignation. 'We're a reputable company in every respect and we value our reputation above all else.'

'But not your employees,' Nick remarked coldly, his anger at the man rising.

'I beg your pardon, Mr Delisantro?'

'You heard me—how long did Eva work for you?'

'Approximately three years,' Crenshawe replied with affronted dignity. Nick could almost see him puffing up his chest.

'And during that time, did she ever do anything like this before?'

'Well, no, of course not. She was a quiet and, we thought, demure employee—we never had any reason to suspect she would—'

'But even so you didn't think she was worthy of a second chance?' Nick interrupted again. The creep had sacked Eva without a moment's notice and by the sounds of it was intending to blacklist her too—and all because she'd succumbed to the explosive physical chemistry between them that even Nick, with all his sexual experience and cynicism, hadn't been able to resist.

'Some things simply aren't excusable,' the man said, but

he'd lost a lot of his bluster and sounded more confused than self-righteous.

'Yeah, right,' Nick sneered, but even as his scorn for the bureaucratic jerk curdled his stomach he knew he had to take a large share of the blame for Eva's predicament.

'So I take it you won't be making a complaint?' the man said tentatively.

'Of course not,' Nick barked, thoroughly sick of the whole situation now.

He hadn't felt this guilty about anything since he'd refused to return to the UK seven years ago and see Carmine Delisantro one last time, despite his sister Ruby's tearful pleas.

He'd done the same thing then that he'd done a week ago. Put himself and his feelings, his wants and desires first, above everyone else's. He hadn't wanted to see Carmine again, because he'd been so bitterly ashamed of how he'd behaved as a teenager towards the man who had raised him. He'd thought at the time it had been the right thing to do, not to risk digging up all that anger and unhappiness and resentment about the miserable circumstances of his birth all over again. But as the years had passed, and he'd never been able to forget Ruby's phone calls, and the funeral invitation that he'd thrown into the trash as soon as he'd received it, he'd finally had to admit the truth. That he'd taken the easy way out. He hadn't done the right thing—he'd just done the right thing for him.

'Well, that being the case, Mr Delisantro,' Crenshawe's voice buzzed in his ear, distracting him from the unpleasant memories, 'I'm eager to talk to you on another matter entirely,'

'What other matter?'

'As I believe Miss Redmond informed you, she was working on the Alegria account.'

Here it comes, Nick thought bitterly. *The real reason for Crenshawe's call.* 'Yeah, what about it?'

'We have reason to believe that Vincenzo Palatino Vittorio Savargo De Rossi, the fifteenth Duca D'Alegria, is your paternal grandfather.' The eagerness in Crenshawe's voice sickened Nick, but he listened.

Maybe he could work this to his advantage. Crenshawe wanted something from him, and he wanted something for Eva.

'I already told Eva, I couldn't give a flying—' He paused, bit back the swear word that wanted to come out. 'I couldn't care less about this duc or his relationship to me.'

'I understand, Mr Delisantro. But I thought you should know that your connection to De Rossi, if it's confirmed, could possibly make you the sole heir to a substantial fortune in Italian real estate and assets. Not to mention the Alegria Palazzo on the banks of Lake Garda.'

'So what? I don't need it,' Nick said, and meant it.

Money had been the driving force of his existence at the lowest point of his life. How to get it had become an obsession that had consumed him every second of every day, so that he could eat, stay clean, stay healthy, find shelter. When you'd been at the very bottom, when the pursuit of a few pennies meant the difference between eating or going hungry, between curling up over a tube grate or having a hostel bed for the night, you discovered just how important money was. And you'd do anything you had to do to get hold of it.

But after he'd clawed his way out of the gutter he'd flung himself into at sixteen, and begun the long, slow and difficult process of remaking himself into the man he had eventually become, he'd made a conscious effort not to let money control his life any more. Sure, he'd pursued it with almost feral intensity long after he'd needed to, but he'd eventually learnt the painful lesson that to get over his past, he had to get over the insecurity of his years on the street, and the 'anything for a buck' mentality that had turned him into a less-than-stellar human being.

He knew that was still a work in progress. His decision not to go and see Carmine Delisantro on his deathbed, and his reckless pursuit of Eva were proof of that. But he had more than enough money now, not just to survive, but to prosper, and he certainly had no need of De Rossi's fortune. Maybe by some trick of genetics he was related to this guy, but he wasn't related to him in any genuine sense.

'But surely, Mr Delisantro, you must at least be curious about the De Rossi family? They are, after all, your blood relations.'

'Look, Henry,' he countered with deliberate insolence. 'Why don't you stop trying to butter me up and tell me what it is you want from me?'

'All right,' the man said warily. 'It's fairly simple really. We've spoken to our client about the results of our research on his behalf.'

'You mean Eva's research,' Nick clarified sharply.

Crenshawe cleared his throat. 'Yes, that's correct, Miss Redmond's research.' The guy at least sounded a little circumspect. 'And the duca would like to meet you. He has requested that you visit his estate in Italy, as a guest, and if things go well he would then involve his lawyers. Of course a DNA test will be required at some point, but he's insisting that he meets you first. On his home turf, so to speak.'

The cagey old bastard, Nick thought wryly. The duca might be looking for a biological heir, but he wasn't going to accept any Tom, Dick or Harry to inherit his precious real-estate fortune, whether they carried his son's DNA or not.

The idea of being inspected and deemed worthy or unworthy by some pompous Italian aristocrat whose own son had been a callow playboy, from the little Nick knew of the man who had seduced his mother, made Nick's temper burn. Who did this duca think he was?

'We'll be sending a representative from Roots Registry to accompany you,' Crenshawe continued. 'To make the introductions and then set out for the duca and his legal team the research we've carried out that supports your claim.'

And to make sure they got their commission out of the old guy, Nick suspected, as he hardly needed an introduction, and any research documents could easily be emailed. But he didn't contradict Crenshawe, an idea forming in his mind.

'When does he want me to visit?' Nick asked.

'As soon as your schedule will allow,' Crenshawe replied, his voice perking up. 'The duca is an elderly man and he wants this matter settled as soon as feasibly possible.'

'And how long does he want me to stay?'

'He's asked for anything up to a month. If things go well, he would like to become properly acquainted with you—and teach you about the holdings you will be inheriting.'

'A month?' Nick almost choked. 'No way. I'm not hanging round in some castle in Italy for a month.' The truth was he didn't think the old guy would want him to stay too long once Nick had given him a few graphic details about his past. This wasn't going to be a heartfelt family reunion, so the quicker they got it over with, the better.

But he was going to go, because he wanted to see Eva again. And if he could get her her job back into the bargain, all the better.

'The final deadline for my latest script is the end of this week,' he continued. And now he had an added incentive to make sure he met it. 'After that there will be rewrites, but that's only after the producers, the director and the lead actors and their agents and assistants and pretty much every other nobody involved with the production company have read it,' Nick added, thinking on his feet, and steadfastly ignoring the little voice in his head that was shouting at him to stop and think this through. 'And it always takes a couple of weeks at least for that to happen.'

'I understand entirely, Mr Delisantro. Of course, we wouldn't presume to impinge on your valuable—'

'Shut up, Henry.'

What kind of pompous jerk used the word 'impinge'?

'I'll book a flight to Heathrow a week tomorrow. Eva can meet me there and you can arrange the connecting flights to Italy. But you'll have to tell your duca I can only spare a fortnight tops. And I want Eva with me at all times.'

He decided not to worry about the fact that the mere thought of having Eva near him again was making heat spread through his system. She might well hate his guts after the way he'd treated her, which would force him to get over her. And if she didn't, well…Two weeks in some luxury palazzo in Italy would be a good way to figure out what had got him so obsessed with her in the first place.

'But, Mr Delisantro, Miss Redmond is no longer in our employ,' Crenshawe said hesitantly.

'That's your problem, Henry. Not mine. But let me give you some advice. If she's not waiting for me at Heathrow a week from tomorrow, you can kiss your commission goodbye.'

CHAPTER EIGHT

Eva reread the monitor in Heathrow's Terminal Five for the fiftieth time and tried to even her breathing. She was starting to hyperventilate.

'In the arrivals hall.' She whispered the words above the hum of conversation and the indecipherable drone of the terminal announcer's voice.

Pulling the two tickets to Milan out of her handbag, she studied the flight numbers for the twentieth time. Then shoved them back in and fastened the bag.

Think pretty thoughts.

But instead of puppies gambolling on a bed of wild flowers springing to mind, the less-than-pretty picture of Nick, his eyes glittering with contempt, leapt into her head. Her breath clogged her lungs, taking on the consistency of treacle.

Breathe.

She pushed out a breath. Gulped in another.

She'd never had a panic attack before, but seeing Nick Delisantro again was exactly the sort of extreme-stress situation that could trigger one. She sucked in several more painfully shallow breaths, exhaled slowly.

Focus. Because quite apart from the humiliation factor, you don't have time to pass out.

Nick's plane from San Francisco was already half an hour late. Their flight to Italy was due to take off in two hours. She had to get them to Terminal One, and ensure they checked in at least an hour prior to take-off. And then…

She swallowed down the lump of treacle cutting off her air supply as heat seeped into her cheeks.

And then she would be spending the next two weeks at Nick Delisantro's beck and call.

She still wasn't quite sure how she'd got into this fix. Everything had happened so fast and so unexpectedly. She'd been scouring the job ads last Tuesday morning, trying to figure out a way to make her meagre savings last while she reinvented her shattered career, her confrontation with Mr Crenshawe not making her feel quite as courageous as she would have hoped, when she'd received a frantic call from her ex-boss—begging her to return to work and claiming that her sacking had all been a terrible misunderstanding. When she'd hesitated momentarily, from shock rather than reluctance, he'd immediately doubled her salary as an incentive.

It was only when she'd arrived at work that afternoon, trying to ignore the inquisitive stares from her co-workers, that she'd discovered the enormous catch in her sudden change of fortunes.

First there had been the astonishing news that she was back on the Alegria account, promptly followed by the heart-stopping information that Nick Delisantro had not only consented to travel to the Duca D'Alegria's estate in Lake Garda, but that he was insisting she accompany him as Roots Registry's representative.

She'd left her boss's office in a daze, her fingers whitening on the printouts of the Alegria client presentation Bob had already started work on, as the whole terrifying scenario had slotted into place.

Nick Delisantro was the only reason she'd got her job back. Mr Crenshawe hadn't had a sudden change of heart, and if she refused to make the trip he would kick her right back out of the door again.

So she'd agreed to go to Italy.

And then endured seven whole days of extreme agitation while she tried to figure out Nick Delisantro's motives. Why had he insisted she go with him? When he couldn't stand the sight of her?

The only possible scenario that had made any sense was that he had devised this trip as some new way of punishing her. As if shouting at her, humiliating her and kicking her out of his apartment weren't enough.

At first she'd panicked. Horrified at the thought of not only having to deal with his anger all over again, but having to spend two whole weeks with him using her as his whipping boy. But after a long phone conversation with Tess, during which she'd given her friend a pared-down version of her one-night stand, Tess had made her realise that she had every right to be mad at Nick and not the other way around.

Unfortunately, despite her show of bravado in finally standing up to Mr Crenshawe, Eva wasn't sure she had enough courage to stand up to someone as dominating as Nick.

The truth was she had even less experience of confrontational situations than she did of sexual ones. As a child she'd always been a champion conciliator, had hardly ever even uttered a cross word at the dinner table—because she'd always been far too aware of the weight of her parents' disapproval if she did. Not that her parents had been bad parents—they hadn't. They'd never been aggressive or unkind towards her, and they hadn't even been particularly strict, except about her schoolwork. But they had never been very affectionate either. They simply hadn't been demonstrative people—and unfortunately she was. She'd longed for the spontaneous hugs and kisses, the casual praise and all those other unconscious signs that demonstrated you were loved and cherished, which she saw her school friends receiving from their mums and dads, but her own parents had never been capable of. And as a consequence of that childhood yearning, she'd become pathetically eager to please. Nick had accused her of always apologising. And he'd been right.

But as Tess had pointed out rather forcefully on the phone yesterday afternoon from San Francisco, he hadn't been right to turn on her the way he had after they'd slept together. He'd accused her of things she hadn't done. Things that, once she'd had a chance to think about it, didn't even make sense. Why on earth would she have needed to sleep with him to tell him he was in line to inherit millions? Surely most people would have been overjoyed to receive that news? The fact that he hadn't been must have something to do with his past.

When had he discovered he was illegitimate? she wondered. Had it been a particularly traumatic experience for him?

Eva frowned at the dwindling line of passengers coming out of the arrival gates, and swallowed down the wave of sympathy.

Don't even go there.

She needed to nurture her indignation and work on her confrontation skills—or Nick Delisantro was going to walk all over her a second time, and the little shards that he'd somehow inserted in her heart would never go away. She definitely did *not* need to feel sorry for him. So making assumptions about what might have happened to him as a child was out.

She peered towards the gate and smoothed damp palms down the lower half of the power suit she'd chosen that morning, after trying on six other outfits. With its knee-length steel-grey pencil skirt, matching tailored jacket and demure white cotton blouse, it made her look one-hundred-per-cent professional.

She was calm now, she noted. Or calm enough. She gripped the handle of her wheel-around suitcase. Her hands had stopped quivering and she was breathing, if not evenly, at least fairly regularly. Once she'd got over this first meeting, established how she was going to play things—calm, detached, not given to emotional outbursts of any kind—everything would be fine.

Then she spotted the tall, well-muscled man strolling out of the gate in a worn T-shirt and low-slung jeans. His caramel brown hair was shorter than she remembered it, hugging his head and curling only slightly around his ears. But there was no mistaking that devastatingly handsome face, the olive skin, or the dark gaze that scanned the crowd, then locked onto her face with a focus and intensity that reminded her of their first meeting.

Her grip flexed and tightened on the handle to stop the trembling in her fingers and the quick, shallow gasp of breath. But it didn't do a thing for the swell of heat beneath her pencil skirt that dampened the gusset of her panties.

She bit down on her bottom lip as he strolled towards her, his strides measured but exact, and the expression on his face completely unreadable.

Ignore the heat. Stay calm, stay professional and, whatever you do, do not say sorry. You're not the one who should be apologising.

She stood rooted to the spot. Determined not to give in to the sudden instinct to lift the hem of the confining pencil skirt and leg it straight out of the terminal building.

She'd flown once before, and he'd caught up with her. What she had to do now was fight.

Fight for composure. Fight to regain her dignity and fight to maintain control of this situation for the next two weeks. Not to mention fight an attraction that for some inexplicable reason had not gone away, despite the appalling way this man had treated her already and the unpleasant way she was sure he intended to treat her again.

Unfortunately, her hormones paid absolutely no attention whatsoever to her mission statement. Because as Nick Delisantro got closer, they began jumping and jigging about as if they'd just won the lottery.

She squeezed the fingers of her free hand into a fist, released them and then thrust out her palm as he stopped in front of her. 'Good afternoon, Mr Delisantro. I hope you had a pleasant flight,' she said, her voice satisfyingly polite and professional despite her jackpot-hitting hormones. 'But I'm afraid we need to hurry or we'll miss our plane to Milan.'

His fingers closed over hers, making electricity zing into her palm and then shoot up her arm.

'*Mr* Delisantro?' One dark brow arched as a mocking smile curved his lips. 'Isn't that a bit formal, given that I've seen you naked, Eva?'

The confidence in his tone, and the spark of humour in his eyes, made it clear he wasn't asking a question. And her temper finally got the better of her hormones.

'Formal works for me, given that you're not going to see me naked again, *Mr* Delisantro,' she fired back, tugging her hand out of his grasp.

Nick chuckled at the steely hint of aggravation in her tone.

Damn, how could he have forgotten how direct she was? And how much he enjoyed that about her?

He let his gaze drift over her, and enjoyed the view too. While the buttoned-up two-piece suit should have made her look a lot less appealing, somehow it didn't. She'd tied her riotous hair back in a ruthless bun, but those big baby blue eyes, full kissable lips and petal-soft skin were as exquisite as he remembered them, belying her attempts to disguise her beauty.

Had she disguised herself especially for his benefit? The thought gave him a nice little ego-boost and confirmed the decision he'd come to on the plane.

He was through feeling guilty about the way he'd lost his temper with Eva the morning after their night together. He'd got Eva her job back—and was submitting to being judged like a prize stallion by a man he'd never met before, plus he was travelling all the way to Italy for the privilege. So as far as he was concerned, his conscience was now clear on that score.

Which had rather neatly paved the way for the second decision he'd come to a split second ago, as his libido had rioted right back into overdrive at the sight of her. He hadn't been able to forget her in two whole weeks now. And he was through trying. They were going to be stuck together in Italy for a fortnight. And he for one couldn't see the harm any more in making the most of it. Especially given that flush of arousal turning her pale cheeks a rosy pink.

'Now that sounds like a challenge,' he teased.

Her eyebrows lifted all the way to her neatly brushed fringe. 'It's not,' she said swiftly, but the firm words were contradicted by the tiny tremble of her bottom lip.

'If you say so, Eva,' he replied, his eyes drawn to her full breasts, which quivered deliciously under the prim shirt she wore.

Heat punched his groin. He wanted to feel the weight of her breasts again. Wanted her straining against him and begging for his touch the way she had a fortnight ago.

That could take a while, he acknowledged, as his thought processes finally kicked in, certainly longer than the first time, given that she didn't seem entirely pleased to see him.

Good thing they had more than one night.

'We have to get to Terminal One,' she said, glancing at her wristwatch and avoiding his eyes. 'The flight to Milan leaves in less than two hours.'

'I'm all yours,' he said, his voice husky with innuendo.

The colour in her cheeks hit critical mass, but she only sent him a wary glance, before shooting off towards the terminal entrance. He followed at a more leisurely pace, easily keeping up with her short strides. And wondered if she realised the tailored skirt did nothing to disguise the seductive sway of her hips.

* * *

He was playing some sort of game with her. That had to be it, Eva thought as she stared out of the aeroplane's small window and the puzzled frown on her face reflected in the perspex.

But she didn't have a clue what game. Why did he keep sending her those long, smouldering looks? And what was with the husky tone of voice? The sexy teasing? Had she imagined it, simply because she was so relieved that he was being cooperative instead of cruel?

She cast a look over her shoulder, to find him lifting his bag into the overhead locker. His T-shirt rose up his waist, to reveal a narrow strip of lean, tanned belly, dusted with dark hair. Her eyes traced the jagged white scar that defined the hollow of his hipbone. And the moisture dried in her mouth, and gushed elsewhere. His arms dropped and the tantalising glimpse disappeared. She squeezed her knees together and jerked her gaze back to the window.

But then her hearing became impossibly acute. She listened to the muffed thump as he sat down, then the creak of the seatback as he adjusted his long legs in the business class seat and finally heard the deafening metallic click of his seat belt fastening.

She stared out at the dull, concrete terminal building, rolled her lip under her teeth.

What was going on? Why was he being so reasonable? He hadn't raised a single objection as she'd rushed them over to Terminal One, dealt with the check-in and then directed him straight to the queue to get through Security.

He'd stood in line behind her for what felt like several millennia but had only actually been about twenty minutes. She'd made some pointless attempts at small talk, until nerves at the penetrating looks he kept sending her had forced her to shut up.

But despite his silence, he hadn't been disdainful, or even annoyed. He'd been relaxed, amused even.

While she felt as if she were on a knife-edge. Why was

she so unbearably aware of his physical presence? Maybe it was simply his height, that imposing physique. She hadn't really noticed how much taller than her he was, until now. That had to be why he seemed to tower over her, why it felt as if he were standing too close. When he really wasn't.

But that hardly accounted for the sudden attack of paranoia. Every time she looked away, she could have sworn she could feel him watching her. The fine hairs on the back of her neck were prickling alarmingly, even now, as if she were being shocked with static electricity. Her brow creased some more in the perspex. She was being ridiculous. A look could not possibly have a physical manifestation. She had to be imagining it.

Soft hairs brushed against her forearm on the arm rest and she jumped. She laid her arm across her lap, and sent him a tight smile to disguise her skittish reaction. 'It's only a two-hour flight. I hope your jet lag's not too bad.'

He sent her a steady look. 'I'll survive.'

'The duca is sending a car to pick us up at the airport. His social secretary said in her email that the drive to his home is about two hours, apparently.'

'Fine,' he said, sounding indifferent.

'What made you change your mind about meeting with the duca?' she asked, on impulse.

His eyebrows lowered slightly, but he didn't reply.

'You didn't seem inclined to pursue your inheritance, before,' she said, trying not to wince at the memory of exactly how disinclined to pursue it he'd been.

'My *possible* inheritance,' he said carefully. 'There's no conclusive evidence that we're related. And I'm not taking a DNA test.'

The reply was deliberately evasive, and only made his decision more confusing. If he had no intention of pursuing this, why was he even going to Italy? 'I doubt the duca will insist on a DNA test,' she remarked.

'Of course he will,' he said, dismissively. 'He'll want proof.'

'He won't need proof once he sees you.'

'Why not?' he said, the hint of irritation surprising her. It was almost as if he didn't want to be related to the duca…

'Your resemblance to his son is uncanny.'

His eyebrows rose fractionally but then his mouth flattened into a thin line. 'I see.' He hissed the words under his breath, just as the steward announced the details of the in-flight services.

'I have a photo of your father, if you'd like to see it?'

Nick looked at Eva blankly. 'My father?' he asked, momentarily confused. Was she planning to whip out the newspaper clipping of Carmine Delisantro? Then he realised who she was talking about, and he had to stifle the renewed stab of annoyance. 'You mean Leonardo De Rossi?'

She blinked. 'Yes, I'm sorry, I meant your biological father. I should have clarified that. I realise this must be hard to—'

'He's not my father,' he interrupted her sharply, not liking the way her features softened.

I don't have a father, he almost added, but didn't. Instead he grabbed the in-flight magazine out of the seat pocket, flipped a few pages to find something to read. But when she took the hint and didn't say anything more on the subject, he began to feel churlish, like a sulky child. Plus biting her head off for no good reason probably wasn't the best way to persuade her he wasn't such a bad guy after all.

He stuffed the magazine back in the pocket. Turned to find her switching off her mobile.

'As far as I'm concerned De Rossi's a sperm donor,' he clarified, careful to hide the bitterness in his voice. 'He means nothing to me. And neither does this inheritance.' He wasn't about to admit that the main reason he'd agreed to come was to see her again, so he added, 'I'm just a bit curious to find out what kind of man could make my mother forget her marriage vows.'

She said nothing for a long time, but he had the strangest sensation she could see right past his show of indifference. The truth was he was more than a little curious about the duca and his son, and why his mother had betrayed his father, or the man he had always thought of as his father, all those years ago.

He felt the unfamiliar flush of colour rise up his neck under her unwavering gaze, then her fingers touched his arm.

'You seem to have a lot of unresolved anger towards your mother.'

'What?' he croaked. *Where had that come from?*

'Your mother,' she said softly. 'You seem to have a lot of unresolved anger towards her.'

That was what he thought she'd said. He gave a half-laugh. 'Is this a joke?'

Her eyes widened as if she was surprised even at the suggestion. 'No, not at all.'

He chuckled, but the sound was hollow. He'd admit to curiosity, but anything else was ludicrous. He propped his elbow on the arm rest to study her. 'My mother died of breast cancer when I was still a kid. Believe me any anger I had towards her for what she did—unresolved or otherwise—is long gone.' He leaned closer, skimmed his thumb across her cheek and watched her eyes darken delightfully. 'Let's talk about something else.'

Her eyes flickered away for a moment, then flicked back to his, the determination in them more than a little unsettling. 'Leonardo wrote a journal, the duca discovered it a year after his death and read it. That's how he found out his son had fathered a child. You should read it,' she said, the earnest tone as disturbing as the sympathy in her eyes.

'No, thanks.'

'It's written in Italian, but I have an English translation if you need—'

'My Italian's fine. I don't want to read it,' he said stiffly.

'But don't you want to know what actually happened?' she murmured, the pads of her fingertips touching his arm again. 'If you read the journal you'll see that your mother wasn't to blame for...'

'I don't care what happened between them.' He tugged his arm off the seat divider. Taking a calming breath, he kept his voice low and even. 'And I never have.'

It wasn't strictly speaking true. He'd cared a lot when he was a teenager, tortured by the thought that his father was not the man he loved, the man he had always tried to emulate, and live up to, but actually some slick Italian playboy who his mother had screwed and then lied about for years.

But he didn't care about it any more. And he certainly didn't want to read about their illicit affair in the playboy's journal. That would just open up all the old bitterness and anger that had followed him around like a bad smell throughout his teens and early twenties, making him do stupid things, take pointless risks—and hurt the only people who had ever really cared about him. He'd finally managed to outrun the anger, finally calmed down enough to make a success out of his life and put all the mistakes behind him—but he'd never be able to apologise to Carmine Delisantro.

The last thing he wanted was to drag any of that guilt up again. Fine, he could admit to mild curiosity about the duca and the man who had impregnated his mother. But he had no intention of playing happy families.

And if that meant he had some unresolved anger, well then maybe he did. But he could live with it just fine. 'Listen, Eva I'm all grown up now, and I couldn't care less about what happened a generation ago between De Rossi and my mother.'

'Okay,' she said, nodding carefully. 'I just thought you might be interested in—'

'I'm much more interested in talking about you,' he cut in, the sudden desire to change the subject almost as acute as the need to wrestle back control of the conversation—and her.

He didn't want to talk about the duca, or his son, or his own past. He was much more fascinated by the woman sitting beside him. And the unprecedented effect she still had on him. Which seemed to have become more acute since their first night. Instead of less.

Even while she'd been asking those intrusive questions, he'd felt the residual hum of arousal at the provocative tilt of her chin, and the softening in her gaze. The small patch of skin where her fingers had touched his arm still sizzled. He'd never been this aware of a woman before.

'What do you want to know?' she asked warily.

Reaching towards her, he drew his thumb across the little indent under her bottom lip, heard her sharp intake of breath. 'Let's start with how you got that tiny scar on your belly?'

As expected the intimate enquiry had hot colour firing across her cheekbones, but her gaze didn't falter. 'It's an appendix scar,' she said, both direct and delightfully flustered.

He leaned close, whispered: 'Want me to kiss it better?'

She didn't reply, but stunned arousal darkened her irises to a rich cobalt as her eyes flew wide.

He closed the gap, caught that full bottom lip between his teeth and gave a soft nip before sliding his tongue across it.

She jerked back, thudding against the aeroplane wall. 'No, I don't,' she said, more breathless than outraged.

'That's a shame.' He chuckled, noting the frantic rise and fall of her breathing, the pink flush on her neck. She fascinated him all right. And what fascinated him most of all was the way she responded to him. And how much her instant, untutored response turned him on.

Even when she was trying really hard not to.

* * *

He kissed me. Why did he kiss me?

Eva rubbed her hand over her mouth, unable to relinquish her fixed stare out of the window.

And why did I let him?

She pressed her lips together where the tiny bite still tingled. The jet taxied down the runway, forcing her body into the seat as it tilted into its ascent.

It hadn't been much more than a playful little nip, followed by a quick brush of his mouth against hers. It wasn't a case of letting him or not letting him. It wasn't that big a deal. She mustn't overreact. This was all part of the game he was playing.

But why wouldn't her lips stop buzzing?

This was worse than she thought, she realised as she heard the ping of the seat-belt sign switching off and her fingers white-knuckled on the arm rest.

Not only did she not have a clue *what* game Nick Delisantro was playing, but she had an awful feeling that whatever game it was, he planned to win.

CHAPTER NINE

THE chauffeur-driven car wound through the carefully manicured hedgerows of the Alegria estate, the red geraniums splashing vibrant colour into the intense green. The duca must have a small army of gardeners, Eva calculated, to keep the flowers blooming in this heat. She slipped open another button on her blouse, careful to keep her body turned to the window and away from her fellow passenger, who'd folded his long body into the seat next to her over two hours ago and promptly fallen asleep.

She'd lost her jacket as soon as she'd been positive Nick wasn't faking sleep to lull her into a false sense of security. Despite the air-conditioning, the sun glaring off the tinted windows, and the overwhelming presence of the man sleeping next to her, had made the interior of the limo stifling. She glanced down at her cleavage, glad to see only the smallest glimpse of flesh and the slight glow of perspiration. She wanted to look as professional as possible when they arrived, and she also didn't want to give Nick any ideas. He'd taken more than enough liberties already on that score. Although quite why he had, she still hadn't figured out.

She risked a look over her shoulder. With his chin tucked into his chest, his arms folded and his long legs crossed at the ankle and stretched out in front of him in the limo's spacious seat well, he'd hardly budged during the journey.

But how could he have fallen asleep so easily?

How could he be so apparently uninterested about meeting his grandfather for the first time? He hadn't asked a single question on the plane about the duca, or her research—or even the estate. In fact, apart from that moment of teasing and the kiss—she pressed her lips together—which she refused to think about again, he'd hardly spoken at all. Instead, he'd opened an expensive laptop not long after take-off and typed at a steady pace, pausing only to order a tomato juice.

When she thought of how absorbing she found tracing the ancestry of people who had been long dead and who she had no connection with whatsoever, she was even more astonished by his attitude. How could he be so calm and composed about meeting a man he was actually related to?

But even as the question echoed in her head she recalled his flat refusal to read Leonardo's journal. To even discuss the man. And the brittle anger in his voice. Maybe he wasn't indifferent about his past and his heritage at all. Maybe he was simply defensive about it. Because discussing the affair between his mother and Leonardo De Rossi brought back painful memories?

She watched him, the vulnerability of sleep making his harsh dominant features look almost boyish, and felt the little blip in her heartbeat at the thought of what he might have suffered when he discovered that Carmine Delisantro was not his father.

The crunch of the car wheels on gravel had Eva blinking back the sentimental thought.

Stop it—you promised yourself you wouldn't do this.

Romanticising Nick's reactions, and reading an emotional response into this visit that almost certainly wasn't even there, would only get her into trouble. She should never have probed about his relationship with his mother, but curiosity, and a stupid desire to soothe the anger she'd seen flash in his eyes, had got the better of her. Nick wasn't a little boy, as he had already pointed out, he was all grown up now. And the secrets of his past were none of her business.

The car swept out of the hedged driveway and rolled to a stop in front of the Alegria Palazzo. Eva sucked in an awed breath, craning her neck to get a better view. She'd seen photographs of the duca's estate, but nothing could have prepared her for the size and grandeur of the structure up close. Wide terraces separated the front of the building from the waterfront. The lake lapped against a wooden dock, where a couple of small sailboats were dwarfed by a muscular scarlet power cruiser.

Multicoloured formal gardens surrounded the mansion itself and stretched towards the forests that rimmed the property. In the distance the Dolomite Mountains created a dramatic natural backdrop to all the man-made splendour, towering over the northern tip of the Lake. She'd done her research on the Ducal Palazzo. Had discovered that it was originally a summer house built on the shores of the lake in the eighteenth-century to take advantage of Garda's pleasant micro-climate and provide the De Rossi family with an escape from the gruelling summer heat of their Tuscan olive plantations. But she hadn't expected anything quite this grand. Obviously a summer house to a duca was a little different in size and magnificence from an ordinary summer house.

Two women in stylish dark-purple uniforms and a man in a matching dark purple suit came out of the palazzo and hurried down the limestone steps that led to the driveway.

Nick hadn't stirred, and she debated whether to wake him, when the chauffeur whisked open her door and bowed. *'Noi siamo arrivati, signora.'*

'Grazie, Paolo,' she said in her rudimentary Italian.

She turned to wake Nick only to find him watching her out of hooded eyes.

'We've arrived at the palazzo,' she said, a bit inanely.

He stretched and then flicked a brief glance out of the

window. 'Yeah,' he murmured. If he was as blown away by the duca's estate as she was, there was no trace of it as he climbed out of the car.

The staff had lined up to greet them, the butler standing so stiff and erect, Eva was half expecting him to salute as she and Nick approached. The man cleared his throat and rattled off a stream of Italian, only some of which Eva understood. Nick replied in the perfectly accented Italian she'd heard him use at the airport, then shook the man's hand and nodded at the two female staff, apparently unperturbed by the way all three of them were gaping at him as if they'd seen a ghost. She would hazard a guess the staff must all have worked for the duca when Leonardo was still alive.

She muddled her way through the introductions with Nick interpreting in short, staccato sentences. For a moment she thought he might be nervous. But he didn't look nervous as he strolled into the house beside her and they were directed to a drawing room just off the entrance hall. The room smelled of lemon polish and old wood, the elegant furnishings as ornate and luxurious as the palazzo's terracotta façade. Floor-to-ceiling shelves loaded with musty leather-bound volumes marked the room out as some kind of library, the partially closed shutters on the casement windows cast long shadows on the tiled flooring. The air felt cool and pleasantly dry after the muggy heat of the outdoors.

A slim middle-aged man in a perfectly tailored suit stood as soon as they entered and walked towards them. He was a few inches shorter than Nick, his clean-shaven jaw and sleek designer clothing in sharp contrast to Nick's worn jeans and day-old stubble. The man spoke in rapid Italian.

Instead of replying in Italian as he had done outside, Nick held up his palm to halt the flow of information. 'You'll have to speak English,' he said firmly. 'Or get a translator. My Italian's not that good.'

Eva blinked, taken aback by the statement. Hadn't he told

her he was fluent on the plane? He certainly hadn't had any difficulty conversing with anyone else.

'I understand, Signor Delisantro,' the man switched neatly into lightly accented English, pronouncing the words with the crisp, clear diction of a natural linguist. 'My name is Luca DiNapoli, I am the head of Duca D'Alegria's legal team. Firstly I must inform you that you are very welcome in Don Vincenzo's home as his guest. But that your invitation here in no way obligates—'

'Silenzio, Luca.'

The gruff words came from behind them. And it was only then that Eva noticed the elderly man sitting at a desk in the far corner of the room. He walked into a stream of sunlight, his patrician bearing as regal and dignified as one would expect from a high-ranking member of the Italian aristocracy.

The familiar golden gaze that Nick had inherited flickered over her face. 'We meet again, Signorina Redmond. A pleasure,' he said, the musical lilt of his accent adding an old-fashioned charm to the greeting. He took her hand, lifted it and then bowed slightly to buzz a gallant kiss onto the knuckles.

But during the whole exchange, his eyes remained fixed on Nick. The mechanical ticks of a carriage clock on the mantelpiece chanted the passing seconds with the deafening crack of rifle fire as the Duca D'Alegria took his time studying his grandson. Slowly, the intelligent, astute, assessing gaze softened, until the rich gold shone with tears.

'Leo.' The old man whispered the name like a prayer, his body trembling.

Eva stepped forward and touched his elbow. 'Are you all right, Your Excellency?' He looked every one of his eighty-eight years all of a sudden, and nothing like the forceful, indomitable and naturally poised man she had met two months ago at Roots Registry's offices.

The duca gave his head a slight shake, then sent Eva a

brief, unbearably sad smile. 'Yes, I am well. Thanks to you, Signorina Redmond.'

Before she had a chance to process his meaning, he collected himself, the moment of fragility vanishing as he addressed his solicitor. 'You may go, Luca.'

The man tried to protest in Italian.

The duca raised his hand. 'We speak in English, Luca, for the benefit of our guests. And don't be foolish. You have only to look at Niccolo to know there is no need for any of that now.' His gaze settled on Nick as he continued to address the other man. 'Leave us, I am tired of your talk. I will contact you tomorrow.'

The solicitor said his farewells. If he was annoyed by the abrupt dismissal, he was well trained in hiding his displeasure.

The same couldn't be said of Nick though.

'Would you leave us too, Signorina Redmond?' the duca asked. 'I would talk to Niccolo in private.'

'She stays,' Nick interrupted before she could answer.

The older man waited a moment, as if assessing his reply, then nodded. 'If you wish.'

'And the name's Nick, not Niccolo,' Nick replied, the cold tone bordering on rude.

The duca stiffened, but instead of ordering Nick to leave, as Eva had half expected, he only inclined his head towards an antique leather sofa and two wide wingbacked chairs, arranged in front of a huge stone fireplace. 'Let us sit. The staff are bringing refreshments.'

'That would be love—' Eva began.

'I don't think so,' Nick cut off her acceptance. 'I've been travelling for close to twenty-four hours. I need to crash for a while.'

As if on cue, the two female members of the duca's staff entered carrying silver trays laden with a coffee service and plates full of dainty sugared pastries and slices of fresh fruit.

Continuing to watch Nick, the duca clicked his fingers and redirected the staff in Italian. The maids left and the butler rushed in, concern etched on his face.

'Eduardo will take you to your rooms,' the duca announced, but the hollow melancholy had left his voice. He sounded stern and his eyes were sharp and completely lucid now as they assessed Nick. 'I dine at nine. Eduardo will show you where.' It wasn't an invitation, but a command from a man who spoke as if he were chastising an errant child, and was willing to be patient, but only up to a point.

Despite the dictatorial tone, Nick shrugged. 'Maybe, if I don't sleep through.'

The reply was insolent, clearly stating that Nick had no intention of obeying the command. Eva had the strangest impression of two stags, one a young buck, the other the leader of the herd, their antlers poised as they prepared to fight for control.

But instead of locking horns, the duca simply inclined his head. 'Eduardo will wake you in good time if you fall asleep, Niccolo,'

Nick sent the old man a hard stare, but didn't reply to the obvious challenge before they were led out of the room by a worried looking Eduardo.

They'd gone a few feet into the lobby area, when a young footman appeared bearing Eva's case. 'Signorina Redmond, we have the room for you in the garden house,' he said in faltering English.

But as she went to follow him Nick took her wrist and she jerked to a stop. 'We're together. I want her in the room next to mine.'

What?

Heat raged up her neck and burned her scalp. She twisted her hand free.

'I don't think that's entirely necessary,' she said to Eduardo, who was already redirecting the footman up the stairs with her case, the mortification on his face plain. 'Anywhere you want to put me is absolutely—'

But before she could say any more, Nick began talking over her to Eduardo in his supposedly rusty Italian. From the look of concern on Eduardo's face and the way he was practically genuflecting to Nick it was clear her protests would be futile.

The Prodigal Grandson had spoken and that was that.

Within minutes, she was being ushered up the wide, sweeping central staircase of the mansion right behind her suitcase, her wishes having been ignored as Nick continued to converse in Italian with the butler.

Not fluent, my butt.

She fumed every step of the way up the stairs to the first floor and then down a long corridor, shock and embarrassment warring with indignation. The footman opened a large door leading onto an enormous room, dominated by a four-poster bed on a dais. Laying her rather worn-looking suitcase on a dressing table, he whipped back the drapes and opened terrace doors onto a wrought-iron balcony that looked out over the lake. Sunlight flooded the room, but the awe-inspiring view did little to calm her rising temper.

Nick had made her sound like his lover.

The footman paused as he crossed back to the door, gave a quick bow. 'Your bathroom is shared with Signor Delisantro,' he said and she was sure she could detect a little Italian smirk of approval. 'This was the room of the contessa.'

Which one? Eva wondered as the footman left, assuming he was referring to one of Conte Leonardo De Rossi's four wives, the last of whom he'd divorced two months before his death. From the grandiose furnishings and the deluxe silken bedspread, she would have guessed the last contessa. A French supermodel who had been under half of Leonardo De Rossi's sixty-five years of age when they had married during a spur-of-the-moment ceremony in San Moritz.

But she wasn't Signor Delisantro's wife. Or his mistress.

In fact she wasn't even his girlfriend. Despite what he'd implied. And she didn't want an adjoining room. Her role here had become completely redundant as soon as the duca had set eyes on Nick. She doubted he would even want to see the PowerPoint lecture she'd worked a week on to explain her research and how she had come to identify Nick's mother as the heartbroken girl Leonardo's journal referred to only *as 'il frutto proibito'*—the forbidden fruit.

Roots Registry would get their commission without her having to prove the validity of her research. And as if her situation weren't already untenable enough, Nick had now made her look like a convenient bit of totty rather than a certified genealogical research fellow. Which was probably all part of the nasty little game he was playing with her.

She unzipped her case and swore under her breath. A word she hadn't used since her teens. Her eyes landed on the bathroom door as she heard the muffled voices of Nick and Eduardo from the hallway. Dumping her treasured collection of lace lingerie into the polished maplewood dresser, she slammed the drawer closed.

The time for playing games was over. She stalked to the bathroom door and sailed through it. Barely sparing a glance for the magnificent marble bath, and the gilded fixtures and fittings, as she headed for the connecting door to Nick's suite. Her hand tightened on the handle.

Forget professionalism. Forget demure, efficient and composed. Forget being a damn conciliator and worrying about stepping out of her comfort zone. She didn't need to put up with Nick's arrogant behaviour a moment longer. She was going to throttle the man.

CHAPTER TEN

Eva gave a quick rap on the door, then marched into Nick's room without waiting for a reply.

She was a rational, level-headed woman who would do pretty much anything to avoid an argument. But she'd never had to deal with anyone as hard-headed, self-absorbed and insensitive as Nick Delisantro before. And there was a fine line between being diplomatic and being a doormat.

And whatever he might believe her role here to be, it wasn't as his doormat...Or as his personal punching bag.

'I want a word with you,' she announced as she stepped onto the thick silk carpeting, and took in the palatial splendour of the master bedroom, which was even bigger than her own suite next door. He stood by the large casement window, with his back to her and his hands dug into the rear pockets of his jeans.

He twisted round, but didn't say anything.

She wrapped her arms round her waist, her temper stuttering slightly under that intimidating gaze. The piercing look in his eyes had little tingles of electricity sizzling across her skin. 'You totally undermined my credibility, my professional integrity and my position here as a representative of Roots Registry by insisting we be roomed together.'

He turned fully towards her. 'Did I?' It was the amused twist of his lips that did it. She felt something inside her crack, and her temper boiled like molten lava flooding through a volcanic fissure.

She strode across the room. 'You know perfectly well you did.' She stabbed her index finger into the centre of the motorbike logo on his T-shirt. 'You made me sound like your mistress. In front of Eduardo and the footman. It was humiliating.'

He pulled his hands out of his pockets and glanced at her finger. She whipped it back, too aware of the unyielding chest muscles beneath.

'And you did it deliberately,' she added, struggling to focus on the lava. 'You… You…' She sputtered, trying to think of a suitable name to call him. Unfortunately, she didn't have a particularly wide vocabulary to hand. She never called people names. 'You…' She racked her brains. 'You berk.'

He gave a rough chuckle and the molten lava burned. 'Berk? Seriously? You need to work on your insults, sweetheart.'

Heat pounded into her cheeks. 'Don't call me that.'

It was the same generic endearment he'd called her two weeks ago. Before he'd kicked her out of his apartment. And she was sure it meant nothing to him. He probably used it with every woman he slept with. But for her it had been special, had made her feel special. And hearing it again now, when all he wanted to do was humiliate her only made her feel more foolish.

'Why not?' he said, apparently oblivious to her runaway temper. 'You *are* sweet.'

He cruised a finger down the side of her face, and she jerked back, the tiny touch like an electrical zap of energy to every one of her pulse points.

'Stop it,' she said, panic making her shout.

He stepped forward, invading her personal space. 'Stop what?'

'Stop playing games with me.' She stood her ground, despite the shock waves of awareness making her whole body tremble and yearn to step towards him—like a vertigo sufferer about to leap off a high ledge. 'It isn't fair and you know it.'

'What games?'

'This game.' She spread her hands, took another step back, the force field of raw machismo pumping off him making the heat pound hotter between her thighs.

How did he do that to her? When she didn't want him to?

'The flirting and the innuendo and the…The kiss,' she babbled. 'The kiss you gave me on the plane. And that look,' she finished in a rush, knowing she sounded like a nutcase, but desperate now to make him stop his little charade. So her body would come to its senses.

'What look?' he asked, but she knew he understood, because he was giving it to her again. Her nipples tightened painfully under the lace of her bra, and throbbed in unison with the tender spot between her thighs.

'*That* look.' She pointed at him. 'That look right there. That says you want me. When we both know you don't.'

The air crackled with tension, and then he had her cheeks in his palms and his mouth on hers.

His lips were firm, warm, seeking and tasted of coffee and need. Without warning, hunger flared, and the craving for him that she'd been pretending didn't exist charged through her system with turbo-powered intensity. He opened his mouth to take more, and her tongue thrust back, drinking him in like a long cold glass of icy water on a hot summer day.

His fingers thrust into her hair as he angled her head to take the kiss deeper—she placed her palms on his waist, her fingers gripping soft cotton and hard muscle and rose on tiptoe, to let him. Searing heat fired through her body as they devoured each other. She wanted him, wanted this, with a power that overwhelmed her.

He stopped first, the breath expelling from his lungs in a couple of ragged pants. She heard her own staggered breathing. Dazed with the sudden rush of sexual hunger and the realisation that she'd forgotten to breathe.

He reached out, pressed his thumb to her raw, swollen bottom lip.

'I'm not playing games.' His thumb trailed down, to where her pulse hammered against her neck, and all she could do was stare blankly back, scared to move in case she swayed towards him like a cat in need of stroking.

His hand dropped away. 'And from the way you kissed me back, I'd say neither are you.'

'We can't do this,' she said. 'It's not appropriate.' The denial sounding absurd after the kiss they'd just shared. But her mind was engaging again, and the stupidity of what she'd just done was staring her in the face. The wild woman had returned.

'Who cares if it's appropriate?' he demanded, his face fierce, his tone tight with impatience. 'We both want to. And we've got two damn weeks here…' She saw it then, the flash of something she would never have expected. Something she'd failed to spot before because she'd been too busy trying to control the uncontrollable.

'Unless I can get His Highness to kick me out sooner.' He turned away, buried his hands back in the pockets of his jeans. But now that her mind had engaged, it wouldn't stop engaging.

'This isn't about me,' she murmured, suddenly understanding the game he had been playing all along. This wasn't a game of humiliation—it was a game of avoidance.

But instead of feeling used, or insulted, all she felt was a choking sense of sympathy. 'I'm just a convenient distraction.'

He glanced over his shoulder. 'You've lost me?'

'It was all an act, wasn't it? That sullen "I don't care about any of this" act you put on downstairs. You're not indifferent, or bored. You're scared.'

* * *

Scared? Was she nuts?

Nick pushed a laugh out past the ball of tension that had lodged in his solar plexus. 'You may be a distraction, but you sure as hell aren't convenient,' he said.

And she'd just become even less convenient.

Why had he kissed her? He hadn't meant to. The plan had been to take things slow and easy, to tease her and tempt her and wait for her to give into her passionate nature again and come to him.

But then she'd stood there in front of him, insisting that he couldn't possibly want her, and all the frustration that he'd been keeping a lid on smashed through the barrier of his will power, and he'd been the one to crack. Not her.

And now he had an erection the size of the Eiffel Tower pressing against the button fly of his jeans to go with his foul mood.

'Stop changing the subject,' she said.

'The only subject I'm interested in is you and me getting naked.' If he'd expected the surly tone to send her packing, he'd been sadly mistaken.

She tilted her head, regarded him with those clear blue eyes that saw much more than he wanted them to. 'Why can't you admit that meeting your grandfather is a big deal?'

He heaved a sigh. Why couldn't she give this a rest? 'Because it's not,' he said, deciding not to correct her once again about the spurious nature of his relationship to the man. Vincenzo De Rossi wasn't his grandfather, any more than Leonardo De Rossi had been his father.

Sure that look of recognition, of stunned affection and hope on the old guy's face in the library had unnerved him. But only because he hadn't been expecting it. And because it had brought with it an unpleasant revelation about his relationship with his mother.

Until Eva had mentioned it, it had never even occurred to him that he might bear a physical resemblance to the De

Rossis. The thought had made him uncomfortable. But what had been worse was the jolt of memory, when the look in De Rossi's eyes had reminded him of what he'd often seen in his mother's eyes. It had been the same damn look of recognition, but with one crucial difference—instead of the hope, the excitement, the stunned pleasure he'd seen in De Rossi's eyes, what he'd always glimpsed in his mother's eyes had been despair and regret. He'd refused to acknowledge it as a boy, had always just strived harder to please her, in the hope that one day she would look at him the same way she looked at his sister Ruby.

His mother had never been cruel to him, never been deliberately unkind, if anything she'd let him get away with a great deal more than his sister, but there had always been this distance between them. Her affection for him had always felt guarded, dutiful, and so unlike the full, rich, boundless love she'd lavished on her husband and her daughter. And he'd never understood why. Until now.

Today, in the Alegria Palazzo's library, while Vincenzo De Rossi had stared at him with tears in his eyes, he'd finally understood why his mother had always found it so hard to love him. Because as he'd grown older, and begun to resemble Leonardo more and more, she would have become painfully aware that he was Leonardo's son. When she'd looked at him, all she had ever seen was the evidence of her sin.

His mother had died years ago, an excruciatingly painful death. She'd told Carmine the truth about his parentage on her deathbed. Two years later he'd run away from home. Unfortunately he hadn't been able to run far enough and the destructive anger—much of it aimed at his mother—had followed him around for years. But he'd eventually come to terms with it and moved on. He'd forgiven his mother—so none of this was a big deal, not any more.

Unfortunately, from the sympathy he could see shining in

Eva's eyes, she was obviously on a mission to share and discuss. Not something he had any intention of doing.

Seeing her mussed hair, and the rash on her chin where his stubble had burned, it occurred to him that there was a much more effective way of changing the subject.

Gripping the hem of his T-shirt, he lifted it over his head and flung it on the bed.

Heat soared in her cheeks, making the tiny sprinkle of freckles across her nose stand out. A spontaneous smile edged his lips. Her eyes had glazed over with stunned arousal, exactly as they had when he'd taken his sweater off in the garage of his apartment two weeks ago.

She might have lived her life like a nun up to now, but the bad girl was well and truly out of the bag, if that look and the kiss they had just shared were anything to go by. All he had to do now was get a stranglehold on his emotions and not crack first again—if he wanted to keep the upper hand in this seduction. And he damn well did.

'What are you doing?' she said. 'We're having a conversation.'

'You may be. I'm not.' He rubbed his palm over his chest. She followed the movement with rapt attention, her tongue peeping out to moisten her bottom lip. The jolt of arousal felt good this time. He was in charge again, in control.

He eased open the first button of his jeans, watched her eyes dart down. 'I'm shattered and I'm taking a shower.' He popped another button.

'You can't,' she said, a little too breathlessly.

His erection swelled back to life under her attentive gaze. 'And after my shower, I'm going to bed.'

'But we haven't finished talking about…' Her voice dried up as the third button went.

'If you want to join me—you're more than welcome.' He ran his hand across his belly, eased his fingers down, under the waistband of his boxers.

Her gaze shot to his face, the colour in her cheeks now radioactive, and the flare of arousal unmistakeable.

'But I should warn you, there's not going to be a lot of talking,' he added.

'I…' She swallowed convulsively. 'I'll see you at dinner,' she murmured and shot off towards the connecting door as if the hounds of hell were snapping at her heels.

The first genuine laugh he'd had all day echoed after her.

Eva Redmond might not be a convenient distraction, but she was a really entertaining one.

CHAPTER ELEVEN

Eva's body was still humming four hours later as she headed through the palazzo's labyrinthine corridors to the terrazzo, where Lorenzo the footman had informed her the duca would be hosting pre-dinner aperitifs for her and Nick.

She wanted to believe it was indignation that had made her throat go dry and other more sensitive parts of her anatomy feel moist and swollen as she'd lain awake on the satin covers of her four-poster, listening to the muffled splash of running water from the bathroom—and imagined Nick Delisantro's naked chest gilded with soap suds—but she wasn't sure indignation quite covered it.

Maybe sexual obsession would be more appropriate. Or complete insanity.

But one thing was certain. She'd always been more comfortable studying the lives and loves of people she didn't know—people in parchment documents, in ledgers of births and marriages and deaths, people who were either long dead or lived lives completely removed from her own. Her life had been exceptionally dull, but also sensible and secure, because she'd never had the guts, or the inclination to take what she wanted and damn the consequences.

Nick Delisantro, on the other hand, didn't have the same reservations. He'd lived his life on the edge and forged a successful career out of taking risks. Which made him extremely dangerous.

Huge French doors lined the airy corridor and opened out onto the estate's vast ornamental gardens. The scent of jasmine and lavender perfumed the air while the dying sun added a redolent glow to the riot of colours.

Eva stared at the lavish gardens and felt the flicker of panic and confusion that had been dogging her all afternoon. Unfortunately, Nick Delisantro's wild, uncivilised behaviour and his reckless approach to life had somehow rubbed off on her.

All he had to do was look at her in that surly, sexy, I'm-going-to-eat-you-alive way he had, and her hormones shot into hyperdrive. She touched her fingers to her chin, felt the slight sting of the mark he had left on sensitive skin.

The low heels of her sandals clicked on the polished stone flooring as she continued down the corridor, frowning into the mirrors that lined the walls. She'd made the stupid mistake of losing her virginity to a man she found it impossible to resist. Even though their one night hadn't exactly been the most comfortable experience, her body seemed to have forgotten the pain.

The sheen of sweat dampened her breasts in the simple summer dress she'd been forced to change into for the evening—because the tailored suit had felt unbearably restrictive. She walked briskly to the open door at the end of the corridor.

She was in serious trouble. Her one wild night with Nick Delisantro had not been a roaring success. The man was taciturn, moody, demanding and unpredictable. And had a temper that she didn't want to be on the receiving end of again. Plus, she'd almost lost her job.

But even knowing all that, everything she knew about herself as a person—her caution, her common sense, her obedience—was on the verge of collapsing around her ears, and she seemed powerless to stop it happening. In fact if the kiss she'd given Nick was anything to go by, all he had to do was take off his shirt and she'd happily fling herself into the inferno again without a second thought.

The only possible solution was to stay away from him… But how could she do that when she was now sleeping right next door to him? For two whole weeks. And he seemed more than happy to exploit her lack of control. She needed a plan, and she had to come up with one fast. Because her will power was non-existent and the rational, sensible behaviour she'd always relied on in the past seemed to go up in flames whenever he was within ten feet of her.

She let out a small sigh of relief when she stepped onto the wide, flagstone terrace situated at the end of the house, and found the duca sitting alone at a wrought-iron table laid with drinks and canapés. She needed to gauge her situation with Don Vincenzo and see if he would be happy for her to fly back to London once she had given him her PowerPoint presentation. She'd considered all the possible permutations, and it seemed like the only option. There was no reason for her to stay longer than a day or two. Don Vincenzo was her company's client, not Nick, so how could he insist she stayed if her job was done?

'Signorina Redmond, you look beautiful,' the duca said in his flawless English as he greeted her with a glass of Prosecco. 'And well rested I hope.'

'Very much so, Your Excellency,' she said, accepting the flute of sparkling wine and the compliment, although she doubted its veracity. She'd had the quickest shower in human history, worried that Nick might walk into the bathroom and press his advantage, and she hadn't managed to get a wink of sleep during her so-called nap. Because she'd been far too busy having inappropriate thoughts about the man in the room next door. 'But, please, call me Eva.'

'Then you must call me, Vincenzo,' he replied, directing her to a bench rimmed with climbing vines that bloomed with purple wisteria. 'My title is little more than an old man's vanity, after all, as we have been a republic in Italy for many years now and rightly so.'

'You're not a monarchist?' Eva said, surprised by the statement. The laws of Italian nobility were notoriously complex and confusing, and fake titles had abounded since the dissolution of the monarchy after the Second World War, but she knew that the Duca d'Alegria's family was one of the few who could claim a direct lineage to the throne—and as such she had expected him to be a strong supporter of pomp and circumstance.

'I am a pragmatist,' he said, the lines of his face more pronounced in the dusky early-evening light. 'My noble title has given me a very comfortable life, several beautiful homes and a pretty crest to put on the bottles of olive oil we produce at the Savargo Estate. And for that I am grateful.' He took the seat opposite her. 'But it did not make me a noble father, nor help me to raise a son I could be proud of.'

'You mean Conte Leonardo?' she murmured, taken aback by the intimate nature of the confidence—as well as the weight of disillusionment in his voice.

'Let us call him Leo,' he said. 'My son always insisted on being addressed by his full title when he was alive. However, he did not deserve it, nor did he honour it, so I refuse to address him by it in death.'

The duca didn't sound bitter or angry, just weary, his voice heavy with regret.

'I didn't realise you had such a low opinion of your son,' she said, feeling desperately sorry for the old man.

'You have read Leo's journal,' he stated. 'So you know my low opinion was well earned.'

She nodded, not sure what to say. How could she argue with the truth? Leonardo's journal had revealed a man who had been given everything he could ever want but who had always wanted more. Reading the translations, she had tried to remain impartial, not to judge, to maintain a scholarly distance while analysing every word and phrase for clues that would help her to identify the young farmer's daughter Leonardo had been introduced to on her wedding day, and then ruthlessly pursued until he got her pregnant. But it had been next to impossible not to despise the author for his arrogance, his reckless pursuit of his own pleasure and his selfish disregard for everyone's feelings but his own. She could understand why a man of principle would find it hard to be proud of such a son.

'Can you tell me,' Don Vincenzo asked, contemplating his glass, 'has Niccolo read his father's journal?'

She shook her head. 'No, he hasn't.' She didn't elaborate, deciding Vincenzo didn't need to know the whole truth—that Nick had refused to read it.

The old man bowed his head. 'So that does not explain his dislike of me.'

'Nick doesn't dislike you,' she countered, her sympathy for the duca increasing. She was beginning to realise that this reunion meant a great deal to the old man, and not just for reasons of heredity. Did he hope to forge a relationship with his grandson to replace the unhealthy relationship he seemed to have had with his son? From what she knew about Nick, she suspected the duca was doomed to failure but she didn't want to add to his pain. 'Nick doesn't even know you,' she continued. 'I just think he's a little overwhelmed by the whole…' She paused, trying to think of a suitable explanation for Nick's animosity. 'By the prospect of the title.' She finished lamely, knowing perfectly well Nick was as disdainful of the duca's title as everything else.

'But Niccolo cannot inherit the title.' The duca lifted his head, concern making his voice crack. 'The rules of primogeniture are clear on the matter. I can only pass the title to a legitimate male heir.'

She had known, and now wished she hadn't said anything.

She laid her hand on Vincenzo's gnarled fingers. 'Don't worry about that, I'm sure Nick doesn't expect—'

'Does Niccolo know he cannot inherit the title?' the duca asked carefully.

'Nick doesn't want the title.'

Eva's head whipped round at the abrupt interruption. Nick stood on the edge of the terazzo, his legs crossed at the ankle and his hip propped against the low stone wall.

How long had he been standing there? From the stark look on his face she suspected quite a while and her heart fluttered uncomfortably. Had he heard her presuming to know what his thoughts and feelings were on the subject of his inheritance? And worse, had he heard Don Vincenzo talking about his son? She was suddenly grateful he hadn't taken her up on her offer to read the journal. While it might help him to forgive his mother, did anyone really need to know they had been conceived in such a reckless, loveless way?

'Niccolo, you have joined us.' The old man stood, his face carefully wiped clean of emotion. 'We are indeed honoured.' The pleasure in Vincenzo's voice was tinged with irony.

Seeing Nick's brow furrow, Eva felt a slight smile tremble on her lips at the evidence of his frustration.

Nick might want to despise his grandfather—and believe he had nothing in common with the man—but she had a feeling he wasn't going to find it as easy as he had probably assumed to deny his heritage. The Duca D'Alegria was a man of honour and integrity, a man for whom family and tradition meant a great deal, but more than that, the man had a sharp intelligence and a dry wit. Surely even a loner like Nick would find that hard to resist?

As the two men continued to spar over Prosecco and canapés it occurred to Eva that she would miss watching the two of them lock horns as they got to know each other over the next two weeks.

But the wistful thought cleared abruptly as the three of

them were led into dinner by Eduardo and Nick's hand settled on her lower back under the pretext of directing her into the dining salon. Heat from the brief touch shimmered through her entire body before she could step out of reach. As Lorenzo the footman held out her chair she looked up to catch Nick's eyes watching her, his heavy-lidded gaze dark with knowledge.

As Eva choked down the first course of asparagus tips wrapped in Parma ham, she let the men's stilted conversation wash over her and studiously avoided meeting Nick's gaze again. She was way out of her depth here.

Nick wasn't vulnerable, or insecure—he was reckless and unpredictable and a dangerous man to get involved with, on any level.

She had to leave the palazzo before she did something monumentally stupid. Again.

'Don Vincenzo, I was wondering if it would be okay for me to return to the UK tomorrow after I've done the client presentation?' Eva heard the clatter of Nick's cutlery but kept her gaze fixed on their host.

She'd waited through their starter, a pasta course of crab linguini, an entrée of rabbit cacciatore and summer vegetables and a dessert of strawberry tiramisu, listening to Nick's monosyllabic answers to all his grandfather's questions, while apprehension tightened her stomach and she struggled to swallow a single bite.

Vincenzo lifted the bottle of wine they had been sharing out of its wine bucket and topped up her glass. His gaze drifted past her to Nick, whom she suspected was glaring at her, but she had to be grateful he hadn't said anything. At last Vincenzo addressed her. 'I never speak of business while I am dining, Eva. It is an Italian's prerogative to do everything in their power not to spoil their digestion.'

'I'm sorry.' The tension stretched taut, but she soldiered on. 'I understand completely, but maybe we could discuss it tomorrow then,' she added hopefully, not wanting to be put off. This was her way out, because she was very much afraid that her resolve wasn't going to stand up to more than one night in the room next door to Nick.

'I have arranged for you to travel to Milan tomorrow to see Luca, while I take Niccolo on a tour of my properties in Riva del Garda,' Vincenzo said easily. 'But once you have shown your research to my solicitors, I see no reason why you should not return to London.'

Eva sent him a tremulous smile. It was a lifeline, if not much of one. Surely she could keep her hormones in check for a couple of days. 'Thanks, that would be—'

'Eva comes with us to Riva del Garda.'

Eva whisked her head round, to find Nick sipping his wine, his gaze willing her to challenge him. 'She can see the lawyers another day.'

'Excuse me, but it's not your decision to make,' Eva said through gritted teeth. How dared he presume to intervene? This was her job. 'It's up to Don Vincenzo when I—'

'Now, now, children.' Vincenzo gave a gruff laugh, holding up his hands to silence her tirade. 'While my grandson's manners could do with improvement,' he said, casting a quelling glance at Nick, 'he is right. There is no rush for Luca to see the presentation. You are more than welcome to accompany us to Riva del Garda, Eva.' Vincenzo rang a small bell, signalling the staff to clear their plates. 'In fact, I insist you come. It is a magnificent little town, full of history. You will enjoy it.'

'It sounds lovely,' Eva said politely, her jaw tense as she realised Nick had managed to manipulate the situation again without even trying. 'And I appreciate the invitation, but I—'

'It is settled, then,' Vincenzo announced, steamrolling over her objection. 'I will inform Luca to expect you another day.'

Eva was forced to nod her assent as her lifeline vanished. 'I'll look forward to it,' she murmured, her jaw so rigid now it was a wonder she hadn't cracked a tooth. It seemed Nick and his grandfather had more in common than just their looks, she thought as Lorenzo whisked away her dessert plate.

'Do you mind if I excuse myself, Don Vincenzo?' she said laying her napkin on the table. She needed to get out of here, before she gave into the overpowering urge to give Nick a good solid whack on the shins under the table. 'I'm exhausted.'

'No of course not.' The old man rose too, shooting Nick another stern look when he remained seated. To Eva's silent astonishment, Nick took the hint and, throwing his napkin onto his plate, pushed his chair back and got to his feet.

As she dashed back to her room through the palazzo's corridors she conceded two things: even if Don Vincenzo managed to teach Nick some much needed manners, he would never be remotely civilised—and she needed a new plan. Fast.

When she reached the bedroom, she flipped the lock, then eyed the connecting door that led to their shared bathroom—which she already knew didn't have a lock.

Dragging an inlaid-gold armchair that stood next to an antique writing desk across the thick silk carpeting, she propped it under the gilt handle, tried the door, then stood back to admire her work. Okay, it was a little desperate and extremely lowering to realise she didn't trust herself to resist that hungry look in Nick's eye should he pay her a surprise visit.

But at least she had a new and brilliantly simple strategy to keep him—and herself—under control. For tonight at any rate.

CHAPTER TWELVE

Rafe's mane of midnight black hair caught the wind, the tempest of emotion on his face as wild and unyielding as the thunderous roar of the sea pounding the ship's deck. 'Ye shall not deny me another night, Shanna,' he yelled. 'I own ye now.'

'Take me then,' Shanna hurled the words through the lashing rain. 'But you shall never own me,' she cried, the fire in her belly igniting as his manhood plunged deep.

Eva groaned and closed her favourite book. It was no good. However hard she tried, instead of seeing Rafe the Pirate Captain and Shanna the fiery beauty who had brought him to his knees, she kept seeing Nick and herself. But Nick wasn't the one being brought to his knees.

Her head shot up at the muffled thump on the balcony. An all-too-familiar silhouette appeared in the open terrace doors. She shrieked and jerked upright in bed—and *The Pirate's Captive* flew out of her hands and landed on the carpet with a thud.

'Nick!' The figure strolled into the room. 'What are you doing?' she squeaked.

'Paying you a visit,' he said, his breathtakingly handsome

face illuminated by the dim light from the bedside lamp. 'What does it look like?'

She leapt out of bed, determined not to be caught lying down, and cursed her own stupidity. Her brilliantly simple plan had a major flaw. The palazzo had no air conditioning, so she'd left the balcony doors open to let the lavender scented breeze from the gardens cool the still air. She'd noticed the neighboring balconies on the bathroom and Nick's room, but hadn't given them a second thought, because they were a good three feet apart. How on earth had he got across? Without breaking his neck?

'You can't come in here.' She headed towards him, deciding to lead with her temper and ignore the pump of adrenaline making her limbs tremble. 'You have to leave.' She thrust her forefinger towards the balcony doors to point him in the right direction. 'Now.'

Instead of following her perfectly succinct order, he walked right past her. 'That's gratitude for you,' he said lazily. 'When I've just risked life and limb to safeguard your reputation.'

She slapped her palms on her hips. *'My reputation?'* she snapped. 'You're in my room in the middle of the night!' she whispered furiously.

Just because her breasts were tingling beneath the skimpy silk of her nightgown, and she'd been imagining him ravishing her on the deck of a pirate ship she definitely did not want him here. 'How is that going to safeguard *my* reputation?'

'No need to get your knickers in a twist,' he countered, the statement making her uncomfortably aware that she had no knickers on to get in a twist. 'No one knows I'm here.'

Before she could tell him that was hardly the point, he gestured to the chair propped against the bathroom door and swore softly. 'I knew it,' he muttered, exasperated. 'You barred the door.' His eyes drifted down her frame. 'Now how childish is that?' he drawled, a slow smile appearing.

Her nipples puckered into hard points, so she crossed her arms over her chest.

'It's not childish,' she muttered, the swelling in her breasts and the pounding between her thighs making it impossible to maintain an adequate level of scorn in her voice. 'Certainly not as childish as climbing about on balconies in the middle of the night,' she added.

He shrugged, picking up the summer dress she'd left flung over a chair. 'I wanted to see you.' He raised the dress to his face and took a deep breath.

She forced down the blip in her heartbeat at the possessive tone, the sensual gesture. 'Well I don't want to see you,' she countered, and tried to make herself believe it.

'What have we here?' he murmured, spotting something on the floor as he flung her dress on the bed. Bending down, he rose holding her discarded paperback. 'Well, well, I never would have guessed it.' He gave a gruff laugh, examining the battered cover—which bore a colourful illustration of a bare-chested Rafe and an all but bare-breasted Shanna in an extravagant clinch. 'You read porn.'

She gasped. 'It's not porn.' She tried to grab the book, but he held it easily out of reach. 'It's romantic fiction.'

He chuckled. 'Girly porn, then.'

'It's not porn of any kind.'

'Let's read it and see.' He held the book down, began to rifle through the pages.

She snatched the paperback out of his hands. 'It's *not* porn,' she said, whipping the book behind her back. 'You'll have to take my word for it.'

No way was she letting him read the book, especially the passages she'd dog-eared. It would only inflame the situation—and her. And her body was already on fire. His big body brushing hers as he backed her into a corner.

Her back hit the wall with a soft thud.

'Eva.' His voice reverberated over her skin as he braced

his hand above her, caging her in, the scent of musk and man filling her senses. 'Why read about it, when you can do it for real?'

'Because I don't want to,' she blurted out, seeing the hungry promise in his eyes as the breeze brushed her bare legs, and a delicious tremble of reaction shimmered down to her toes.

He touched his lips to her ear lobe, and whispered: 'You're lying.'

She opened her mouth, but the denial got stuck in her throat. She could feel the slickness of her sex, the tenderness of her breasts, hear the rasp of her own breathing.

One rough palm settled on her leg, cutting off her air supply completely. Her thigh muscles quivered and bunched, her breath expelling from her lungs in a rush as his hand trailed upwards.

'You want to know how I can tell you're lying?' he murmured.

She shook her head, but revelled in the zing of sensation as his callused palm rose up her leg.

His thumb brushed across her hip and traced the top of her thigh. She shuddered, her fingers releasing the paperback, the gentle thump as it hit the floor barely registering as his thumb dipped into the curls covering her sex. 'You're wet and ready for me right now, aren't you, Eva?'

'Please…' she begged as longing blazed through her. She *was* wet, and ready. Ready to forget everything. Her job, her sensible well-ordered life, her sanity, if only he would touch her more. Touch her there.

He bit into her ear lobe, the sharp nip a delicious counterpoint to the painful shock of pleasure as his thumb found the perfect spot at last and rubbed.

She sobbed, clutching the muscle of his bicep, and clung on, riding his stroking thumb to increase the torment. Her wollen breasts arched into his chest as the orgasm swept through her in one tumultuous, all-consuming wave.

She forced herself to let go of his arm as she drifted back to her senses. She pressed back into the wall, knees still weak from the intensity of her climax. But instead of the smug expression she had expected, all she saw in his face was fierce lust burning the golden brown of his irises to a molten chocolate.

'I rest my case,' he rasped, lifting his thumb to his lips and licking.

'You're right,' she said, her voice as shaky as her legs. 'I do want you, but you scare me too.'

Was what she felt for him more powerful, more overwhelming than simple lust? She swallowed heavily, looked away from his penetrating gaze, ashamed of her own cowardice, and worse, terrified that he would see the yearning in her eyes. And realise how needy she was.

He lifted her chin, and her eyes met his, the tenderness and concern in them making the frantic beat of her heart increase. 'Don't be scared, Eva,' he said gently. 'I won't take you until you're ready. Not this time.'

'What do you mean?' she said, confused by the note of self-loathing she detected.

He stepped back, huffed out a breath. 'I did that once before and look what happened. You lost your job.'

'That wasn't your fault,' she corrected, more confused than ever. What was he saying? That he felt responsible for her losing her job?

'Whatever.' He shrugged. 'The point is, it doesn't matter now because you've got it back.' The words were delivered in an offhand manner, as if the information was irrelevant, but as soon as he said them something she had never understood suddenly became blindingly obvious.

'Oh, my goodness!' She pressed her palm to her mouth, her shock as real as the disturbing rush of emotion at the thought of what he'd done. 'That's why you agreed to come here. That's why you changed your mind about meeting your grandfather. To make Mr Crenshawe give me my job back.'

She'd thought he'd done it out of some vindictive desire to punish her, when what he'd really been doing was helping her.

He gave a strained laugh. 'Yeah, like I'm really that noble,' he said, but she wasn't fooled.

'But you are,' she said, all the more convinced because of his attempt to deny it. 'You didn't have to insist I accompany you. But you knew Crenshawe would have to re-employ me if you did.'

'Stop being so naïve,' he said, frustration sharpening his voice. 'I engineered this whole thing so I could have you again. You getting your job back was just a nice fringe benefit.'

'I don't believe you.' She thought of his defensiveness when she'd spoken about his mother. His prickly response to his grandfather. And the emotions swirling in his eyes when she'd confronted him that afternoon. Why would he go through all that just to sleep with her, when he could have any woman?

'Yeah, well, you should.'

'You did something good. Something kind and sweet,' she shot back. 'Why is that so hard for you to admit?'

He swore, flattening her body against the wall. 'Because, damn it, I'm not kind and sweet.' Large hands grasped her waist, lifting her, until the long, hard ridge in his jeans pressed against her. 'Feel that—that's what I want from you. That's the only reason I'm here.'

Firecrackers of need exploded in her sex at the memory of his thick girth lodged deep inside her, stretching pain turning to blinding pleasure.

She writhed and he gave a harsh laugh. 'I'm not one of the good guys, Eva. Remember that,' he snarled, his erection grinding into the juncture of her thighs. 'But I'm going to wait for you to come to me this time. So you know exactly what you're getting into.'

He let her go.

'But I already know,' she said, the words shuddering out on a shocked sob.

'No, you don't.' He ran his thumb down her cheek. 'Because you're way too sweet and naïve for your own good.' Tucking his forefinger beneath her chin, he raised her gaze to his. 'Sex is all I'm looking for. There aren't going to be any hearts and flowers like in your book. Not with me. And I want you to understand that before we go any further.' He placed a firm, possessive kiss on her lips. 'Now go get me Leonardo's journal.'

'I… Why?' she stammered.

'I need something to help me sleep. And your girly porn isn't going to cut it.'

She nodded, skirting around him, and then crossed to the antique dresser, her thoughts whirring at what he'd revealed. Why was he so convinced he was one of the bad guys?

She pulled the leather-bound book from her suitcase, handed it to him.

Her heart plummeted at the sight of his long fingers closing over his father's diary. Reading the truth of that cruel, long-ago seduction would only make this trip harder for him.

'I'm afraid I only have the original,' she said and bit back the urge to snatch the journal from him, knowing he would only scoff at her concern.

He flipped the book up, caught it one-handed. 'That's okay.' He touched the spine to her cheek, trailed it down her throat, and traced the neckline of her gown, her bosom rising and falling in jerky spasms. 'Get a good night's sleep, Eva Redmond.' A suggestive grin flashed across his handsome features. 'Because it may be your last.'

She gave a nervous little laugh as he walked through the terrace doors, clamping down on the urge to call him back.

To tell him to finish what he'd started, that she wanted him now, that she was ready.

The wrought-iron railing creaked as he jumped onto the balcony and disappeared into the night. She returned to her empty bed, climbed beneath the sheets, and turned off the bedside lamp.

Nick Delisantro wasn't right about himself. He was a better man than he believed himself to be. And he wasn't right about her either. She wasn't naïve, she was only inexperienced. And just because she got a vicarious pleasure from reading about virile pirate captains and their beautiful captives, she did know the difference between fiction and reality—thank you very much.

But he was right about one thing. She needed time and space to analyse her feelings, to consider the situation rationally and sensibly before she did something wild and reckless again—and then discovered she couldn't control the consequences.

CHAPTER THIRTEEN

The smell of her arousal makes me hard. She's begging for it. Her husband is a fool, and as inexperienced as she is, he can't satisfy her, so I will. And afterward she'll always wish it was me between her thighs and not him.

Nick slammed the book closed and growled out a guttural expletive, his fingers digging into the worn leather.

What a creep.

He slung the journal onto the coffee table. If he'd learned one thing over the last two sleepless nights waiting for Eva to come to him, apart from the fact that he was his own worst enemy, it was that Conte Leonardo Vittorio Vincenzo De Rossi had been a lecherous, egotistical, misogynist jerk who had about as much restraint as a horny schoolboy and a lot less literary talent.

Nick levered himself out of the armchair and stalked across the bedroom to the balcony. The night air was still and silent but for the quiet chirping of some unknown insect. He took a deep breath into his lungs. The perfumed scent of the garden's flowers mingled with the fresh scent of lake water and went some way to clearing away the stench that clung to him after reading Leonardo's grubby little secrets.

The light spilling from Eva's open terrace doors had the

last of the grim thoughts clearing away to be replaced by a healthier frustration.

Shoving his fists into the pockets of his sweat pants, he leaned back against the balcony rail, and contemplated his own stupidity. And the miserable thought of spending another torturous night without Eva's lush little body under his.

Why had he said he'd wait for her to come to him?

Then the image of her trusting blue eyes, wide with confusion, and her body trembling with arousal yesterday evening came back to him. And he knew he hadn't had much of a choice.

She'd responded so beautifully, come apart so easily in his arms. After the smallest of touches she'd been wet for him, pleading for release. When she'd climaxed, he'd been so close to burying himself up to the hilt and satisfying both their hungers that it was making him hard just thinking about it.

But then she'd whispered that line about wanting him, but being scared of him too—and his conscience had as good as kicked him in the nuts.

She'd sounded so young and so impossibly vulnerable. And things had only got worse when she'd got some insane idea into her head about him coming to Italy to get her her job back, when his motives hadn't been anywhere near that pure. And then started spouting loads more nonsense about him being a nice guy. Nonsense he could see she actually believed.

He braced his hands on the balcony, stared out into the night, his frustration making the muscles in his shoulders throb.

Him? A nice guy? Hardly.

The woman had led a seriously sheltered life if she believed that. She'd certainly read way too many of those racy books that peddled all that happy-ever-after stuff and made women think that hot sex equalled love.

He gave a harsh laugh. As if real life were anything like that. He propped his butt against the balcony rail, alert to even the slightest sound from her room. But all he heard was the cricket going berserk and the water lapping on the dock below. His nose wrinkled, the citrusy aroma of lemons floating up from the tree under his balcony reminding him of the sharp, fresh scent of Eva.

He dropped his head back and gazed at the stars sprinkling the night sky, the tension in his shoulders almost as pronounced as the tension in his groin.

But wasn't that just the problem with Eva? She hadn't had a real life, not yet anyway. How could she have and still have been a virgin at twenty-four?

He let his chin drop and cursed. Which was why he had to treat her with a little more care than any of the other women he'd slept with. Not only did she not know the score, she probably didn't even know there was a score.

He knew how much she wanted him. That sure as hell wasn't in any doubt. If it hadn't already been obvious after her live-wire response to his caresses last night, it had been even more so today during their scheduled trip to Riva del Garda.

He'd heard her strangled little gasp when his thumb had lingered on the inside of her elbow as he'd helped her into the duca's motor launch. Had smelt the glow of sweat forming on her nape when he'd stood just a little bit too close as they were escorted round the duca's riverside offices. Had felt her body quiver when he'd stroked his palm down her spine, and left it resting above the curve of her buttocks to direct her to her seat in the waterfront restaurant Don Vincenzo had booked for lunch. Had seen the way her eyes darkened when he'd brushed a lock of silky hair behind her ear during their pre-dinner drinks at the palazzo.

Truth was, he'd been so damned attuned to every one of her responses—every single sight, scent, sound and touch—he'd actually been grateful to have the duca there chaperoning them, or he wouldn't have been able to stop himself dragging her off and forgetting about his stupid promise altogether.

The woman was driving him mad. He'd never been particularly good at deferred gratification. And he was getting less so every second he spent in her company. Even now he could taste the sultry scent of her arousal, hear her shocked gasp as he circled the stiff nub of her clitoris.

The blood pumped into his groin. His teeth clenched and his back muscles knotted as he spent several fraught moments contemplating the quick journey from his balcony into her bedroom—and the feel of soft, slick skin, dewy with need.

Damn it, Delisantro, get a grip. You're worse than Leonardo.

The repulsive thought doused the fire like a bucket of icy water. He sucked in a breath, pushed out another, thrust shaking fingers through his hair, and shoved away from the balcony to head back into the bedroom. Sick loathing made his stomach muscles clench when he spotted Leonardo's journal on the coffee table.

Stop torturing yourself.

Stretching out on the bed, he punched the pillows into submission and switched off the bedside lamp. He had no connection to Leonardo. So what if he looked like the guy? He had more than enough sins of his own to deal with, without shouldering the blame for someone else's.

Folding his hands behind his head, he watched the moonlight cast eerie shadows in the velvet canopy above his head and waited for the nausea to go the hell away. The light citrus-scented breeze gradually cooled the sweat on his brow and replaced the acrid taste in his mouth, bringing with it comforting memories of Eva. And her nutty insistence that he was a nice guy.

Welcome heat curled in his abdomen.

No, he wasn't a nice guy. Or a particularly patient one. But he'd proved that he could be decent, or decent enough, by giving her some time to realise he wasn't one of her storybook heroes.

That said, he wasn't a masochist—which meant he'd be

doing his very best tomorrow to ensure he didn't have to spend any more nights alone with only Leonardo's creepy journal for company.

CHAPTER FOURTEEN

'Your mind is elsewhere today, Niccolo?'

Nick glanced up from his lunch, to find Don Vincenzo's astute gaze steady on his. He sighed inwardly. He'd stopped bothering to correct the old guy about his name yesterday, when he'd figured out the man was as stubborn as he was. And yeah, he was a little preoccupied all right.

He hadn't expected Eva to be gone this morning before he'd woken up. He also hadn't expected her to sneak off to the lawyers' offices in Milan without bothering to mention it to him. But worse had been the panic that had skittered up his spine when he'd found her room empty at ten o'clock and figured she'd run off back to London. He'd felt pretty stupid about that when Eduardo had told him the truth. But that hadn't stopped him sulking for a while, and then watching the clock all morning waiting for her to return.

Make that a lot preoccupied.

But he wasn't about to talk to an octogenarian he barely knew about the dismal state of his sex life.

'I guess I'm still jet-lagged,' he muttered.

Don Vincenzo nodded, as if digesting the information, then said: 'Eva tells me you have read my son's journal.'

Nick put down his fork. 'Yeah. Some of it.' Where was this headed? Because talking about Leonardo's journal was even less appealing than talking about Eva's disappearing act.

'So now you know—' Don Vincenzo's hand shook as he laid his napkin on the table '—that I raised a vain, self-absorbed man, who preyed on women simply because he could.'

Nick hitched a shoulder. 'I guess,' he said, wishing he couldn't see the pain in the old man's eyes.

'I owe you an apology, Niccolo, on behalf of the Alegria family.'

Nick stiffened. 'It's not your job to apologise for what he did.'

'I was his father, I should have—'

'And anyway, I don't need an apology.' Nick interrupted, hoping like hell to put an end to the conversation. 'I did okay.'

He hadn't wanted to like Don Vincenzo. Hadn't wanted to feel anything for the old man at all. But it was proving next to impossible not to.

He knew what the old guy wanted. Had figured it out yesterday as Don Vincenzo had squired Eva and him round his properties in the picturesque town of Riva del Garda and spoken with pride and hope thickening his voice about the estates and businesses he owned in Tuscany.

Don Vincenzo was looking for someone who would care about the Alegria legacy and the various properties and businesses he had nurtured and watched grow for the last forty years. But more than that, the old man wanted a grandson who would love and respect him, to replace the son who never had.

And Nick simply wasn't that guy. His life was in San Francisco, where he wrote about the dark underbelly of urban life, because he'd once been a part of it himself. He didn't know the first thing about managing a business, or the day-to-day running of an ancestral estate. And he didn't do love and respect either. He didn't want to be a part of Don Vincenzo's family, because he hadn't shared that connection with anyone. Not since he'd been a kid. And look what a staggering success he'd made of that.

'How can you say that?' Vincenzo asked dispassionately. 'When you ran away from home?'

Nick flinched. 'How do you know about that?' he asked, but he could already guess. Don Vincenzo was a shrewd businessman, of course he would have had him investigated.

Don Vincenzo bowed his head. 'When Henry Crenshawe informed me of your name, I endeavoured to find out all I could about you.' Anger flashed in Vincenzo's eyes. 'Why did you run? Did Delisantro reject you after he found out you were not of his blood?'

'You've got it all wrong.' A shame Nick thought he'd buried years ago lurched back to life. 'Carmine Delisantro was a good man and a great dad, but when I found out about…' He paused. Why couldn't he say Leonardo's name? 'I rejected Carmine, not the other way around. So if anyone needs to apologise it's me.'

'You were a boy.' Vincenzo sighed. 'No child should have to find out what you did. If the man who raised you was as good a man as you say, I'm sure he forgave you.'

'He did.' To his horror, Nick felt his voice crack. He stared at his plate, recognising the grinding pain in his stomach for what it was. Guilt.

Carmine Delisantro had forgiven him all right, and he'd carried on loving Nick right up until his dying day. But Nick had been too much of a coward to admit he felt the same. So what did that say about him?

Don Vincenzo's hand covered the fist Nick had on the table. 'I will be travelling to Milan tomorrow to change my will. As you know, to my great regret I cannot pass the title to you, because you are not a legitimate heir.'

'There's nothing to regret. I don't want the title.' Nick's fingers released and the grinding pain began to dim. Thank goodness, the old guy had finally realised Nick wasn't cut out to be anyone's grandson.

'Very well, then.' Vincenzo patted the back of his hand and

sent him an easy smile. 'I have a second cousin in Palermo who shall become the sixteenth Duca D'Alegria.' The man's lips quirked in a benevolent smile. He gave the ornate dining room a quick survey before his gaze fixed back on Nick. 'But to you, Niccolo Carmine Delisantro, I shall take great pleasure in leaving the rest of my estate and the Alegria Palazzo.'

'What?' Nick's shoulder muscles spasmed as he leapt out of his chair. 'Why would you do that? You don't even know me. I told you I don't want—'

'Sit down, Niccolo, and stop panicking.' To Nick's astonishment the old man simply laughed, the sound gruff and genuinely amused. 'My doctors tell me I have a few years yet before you need worry about receiving this gift.'

'But damn it, I don't want your gift.' He slapped his palms on the table, rattling the plates. 'And I sure as hell don't deserve it.' The thought terrified him. Not just the responsibility he would have to maintain the land, to manage the staff and the property and the businesses, but also the connection, the debt he would owe to the man.

Instead of looking appalled, or even annoyed by Nick's outburst, Vincenzo cocked his head to one side, his oddly penetrating gaze disturbing Nick even more. 'Why would you think you don't deserve it?'

'Forget it,' Nick replied, the panic starting to choke him. He didn't have to explain himself to Don Vincenzo or anyone else. He'd made his own life, free of family, free of emotional ties and that was the way he intended to keep it. 'I don't want this inheritance. And you can't make me take it,' he said, slinging his napkin on the table and turning to leave.

'We shall talk of this later, when you have calmed down...'

The buzzing in Nick's head drowned out the rest of Don Vincenzo's words as he strode across the room, desperate to escape from the misguided hope and affection in the old man's eyes.

He knew he sounded like an ungrateful kid, the same ungrateful kid who had once thrown everything away that mattered because of pride and temper and stupidity. But so what? The past was gone. He couldn't go back and change it. Any more than he could change who he had become.

He raised his eyes from the floor and stopped dead at the sight of Eva standing in the doorway, her hands covering her mouth, her blue eyes round with sympathy.

The silk-papered walls of the elegant parlour rushed towards him.

How much had she heard?

His vision dimmed, the sudden claustrophobia forcing him to move.

'Nick, are you all right?' she whispered, reaching out.

'I'm fine.' He shrugged off her fingertips as he strode past her, through the palazzo's marble lobby and straight out of the entrance doors. The burning heat of the afternoon sun did nothing to dispel the shocking chill creeping into his bones.

He was running away all over again.

But he had to get out of here, get away from his grandfather's misguided trust—and the sparkle of distress on Eva's lashes.

CHAPTER FIFTEEN

'Nick, come back.' Eva rushed down the steps of the palazzo after Nick's retreating back. Kicking off her heeled sandals, she left them on the hot stones and ran barefoot, desperate to catch him as he headed towards the dock at the end of the waterfront.

She hadn't meant to eavesdrop. Hadn't meant to listen in to what was clearly a private conversation. But when she'd entered the pleasantly cool lobby after her exhausting trip to Milan, she'd been flushed with pleasure at the sound of the muted voices coming from the dining salon. How wonderful to hear Nick finally conversing with his grandfather in full sentences. But then she'd stood in the doorway, heard the raw emotion in Nick's voice, had actually registered the words—and been stunned into silence.

Why was he so angry and upset at the thought of inheriting the Alegria estate? And why would he think he didn't deserve it?

The crippling sense of responsibility had hit her first. Nick had come to Italy to help her get her job back. But that had been swiftly followed by the desire to soothe the hurt and panic she had seen in his face.

He'd looked stunned and had clearly been horrified she had witnessed his outburst. But how could she ignore his pain and confusion now she had?

Seeing him step onto the cherry-red power cruiser moored at the end of the dock, she picked up the hem of her skirt and ran down the worn wooden boards.

She could help, but only if she caught up with him.

'Nick, hang on.' She skidded to a halt on the dock, panting as the duca's dock keeper released the thin nylon line mooring the cruiser to the quay. 'Where are you going?'

'For a ride.' He caught the line the dock keeper threw across. 'Alone.'

After sending a perfunctory salute to the man beside her, and tying off the line, he crossed the boat's deck and leapt up the steps to the pilot's cabin.

The powerful boat kicked to life, water churning as it glided away from the dock. Without taking time to think about it, Eva took two steps back, and then ran at full pelt, squeezed her eyes shut and launched herself off the dock and into mid-air.

The soles of her feet slapping on the deck were accompanied by the alarmed shout of the dock keeper. She pitched onto her knees then grabbed onto the handrail, her knuckles whitening as the boat lurched forward.

Okay, that wasn't the most graceful thing she'd ever done, but at least she hadn't drowned.

Fighting the sway of the boat as it rode the swell, she clambered up the steps to the cabin.

Nick glanced at her, a dark scowl on his face as he swung the boat's steering wheel into a turn to direct the boat onto the open lake. 'You little fool, you could have hurt yourself.'

'You could have waited for me,' she said, unperturbed by his reprimand, and perched on the leather bench seat behind him.

With his legs akimbo, his T-shirt moulded to his muscular chest and his caramel brown hair whipping about his head he looked savage and uncivilised. Like a pirate captain at the bow of his ship, ready to maraud and pillage anything that took his fancy.

Eva shook off the fanciful thought. This wasn't a romantic fantasy. It was real life. And she wasn't scared of Nick. Not any more.

'I wanted to be alone.' He glared at her, a muscle in his jaw twitching as his gaze narrowed. 'What part of that didn't you understand?'

She clutched the leather cushion as the boat skimmed over the wake of a couple of wind-surfers and rounded the point, leaving the cove that sheltered the palazzo behind. 'You don't always get what you want.'

Nick let out a harsh laugh. 'You don't say,' he murmured, his voice thick with innuendo as his gaze flicked to her cleavage.

Eva's cheeks hit boiling point, awareness shimmering, but she refused to rise to the bait. He was trying to provoke her. And divert her attention.

She touched the soft hair of his forearm. 'What are you so upset about?'

The sinews in his arm tensed, and the muscle in his jaw bunched. But that was his only reaction to the question.

He grasped a lever on the dashboard, which looked like a throttle. 'You wanted to ride,' he said, yanking the lever down. 'So let's see what this baby can do.'

The engine roared, lifting them up and throwing Eva back against the seat. Then the boat powered across the water as if catapulted out of a sling, skimming over the choppy surface as they shot towards the sun. Eva's bottom bounced on the bench, the wind and spray refreshing as she screwed up her eyes and held on tight, the punch of adrenaline making her heart pound.

Nick stood, his hands gripped on the steering wheel as he negotiated the leisure traffic with practised ease.

He looked fierce, indomitable. And yet she'd seen the

moment of vulnerability when his gaze had met hers in the dining salon. Meeting Don Vincenzo, learning about his biological father had been hard for him. Probably much harder than he had imagined or would ever admit. And her heart went out to him, even if he didn't want it to.

Minutes passed as they drove to the far end of the lake, leaving the crowds of smaller craft and the heavily developed shoreline behind. Heading back into the shallows, the boat rounded a rocky outcropping and entered a quiet cove. The engine slowed as they approached a ramshackle dock that listed to one side. A stone shrine topped with a crucifix nestled among the plants and bushes edging the water.

She had no idea where they were as Nick eased the throttle down and the boat kicked and settled in the water. But wherever they were, they were alone. The gentle lap of the water on the powerboat's hull the only sound above the rasp of her own breathing. She could feel the prickle of heat and anticipation shimmering over her skin, the mist from their ride dampening her cotton blouse but doing nothing to cool the heat pulsing through her veins. His hooded gaze locked on her face, the fine spray of water on his hair sending it into unruly furrows as he whisked it back from his forehead.

He looked wild and untamed, the anger when she'd jumped on board replaced by fierce arousal. But the harsh desire on his face didn't frighten her, because she'd had time to think about what she was letting herself in for.

Nick wasn't looking for love or commitment. But then neither was she. He was a complex man, who guarded his feelings and his vulnerabilities and, she suspected, found it next to impossible to trust anyone because of the circumstances of his birth. She'd really have to be a romantic fool to think that she, with her limited knowledge of relationships, could have any hope of changing that.

But that didn't mean they couldn't share something worthwhile together for the short time they had. He'd warned her that this could only ever be a purely sexual adventure. But she already knew it was more than that. Because whatever Nick wanted to believe, she already cared about him, and he cared about her.

Propping his butt on the control panel, he crossed his legs at the ankle and beckoned her with his forefinger. 'Come here,' he said, his voice husky with hunger.

She stood still, the desire burning.

Leaning forward, he hooked his forefinger in the waistband of her skirt and yanked. 'I said, come here.'

She stumbled towards him, flattened her palms on his chest. Rough, urgent hands lifted her skirt, caressed her thighs and moulded her buttocks, his lips fastening on her throat, his teeth nipping at the place where her pulse hammered.

She dropped her head back to give him better access, ground her backside into his palms, whispering: 'I thought you wanted to be alone?'

'Not any more,' he growled, the demand urgent in his voice. Rough hands snuck under the waistband of her panties, then ruthless fingers found the zip on her skirt and dragged it down.

She looped her arms round his neck, hoping he couldn't feel the quiver of trepidation as he sat on the bench seat and yanked her down to straddle his lap.

She grasped his shoulders as he captured her mouth. Moist heat flooded between her thighs, his erection confined by soft denim rubbing against the damp cotton of her panties as she let the hunger that had built in the last two days consume her.

She rode his length, revelled in his staggered breathing and threaded her fingers into the hair at his nape. Then urgent seduction turned to violent need. He ripped at her blouse, buttons popping. She dragged his T-shirt over his head, exploring the ridged steel of his abdomen, the velvet steel of his chest.

The brown of his irises darkened before his mouth covered her breast through the delicate lace of her bra. She cried out, the keening sound of pleasure echoing away on the breeze as he tasted and teased with his teeth, then suckled strongly. Eva bowed back, arching into his mouth to feel more, to take more. Clever fingers released the bra's hook, peeled away the wet lace. She shivered, the nipple tightening, swelling. His lips feasted on naked flesh: hot, hard, perfect.

She lost focus, delirious with longing and exhilaration. He needed this, needed her as much as she needed him.

He swore softly, banded his arms round her waist. 'Hold on,' he croaked, lifting them off the bench together. 'We're taking this below deck.'

She wrapped her legs round his waist, clung on, as her dazed brain registered the rumbling hum of a passing speed-boat. He staggered down the steps into the boat's cabin, then strode through the galley to the bedroom.

She landed on the wide double bed that took up most of the compact space. Rising on her elbows, she watched him kicking off his deck shoes, struggling out of his jeans and boxer shorts, then grabbing a small foil packet from the back pocket.

Her breath expelled in a rush. He looked magnificent. But she wasn't worried any more. Rising on her knees, she touched the powerful erection. Marvelling at the hardness, she cupped the generous weight of him in her palm.

Gazing up, she met eyes ablaze with arousal. 'Can I kiss you there?' she asked.

'No,' he groaned.

He threaded her fingers through his, pulling them away from his flesh before he rolled on the condom.

He climbed on the bed, forcing her back. Cradling her cheek, his fingers trailed down her neck to stroke the curve of her collarbone. 'Later,' he murmured. 'Or this is going to be over way too soon.'

His hand shaped her breasts, caressed her hip, cradled her buttocks, then long, talented fingers delved into the wet curls at her core.

She bucked, clamped her knees together, the shocking touch almost more than she could bear.

'Open for me,' he urged.

Her knees weakened, loosened for him of their own accord. He rubbed, stroked, circled the burning nub. She heard her own broken sobs as his fingertip skimmed over the heart of her. She cried out as the slick heat built to an impossible crescendo. She couldn't breathe, couldn't think, but as she clung to that desperate edge, her senses screaming, she knew this wasn't how she wanted it. Not this time.

She closed her legs, shivered against him. 'Please...I want you inside me.' She choked out the bold request.

He rolled onto his back, pulling her with him, forcing her to spread her legs and bracket his hips. 'Then I want you on top,' he demanded.

Large hands cupped her buttocks, directing her to his shaft and then he drew her down. She shuddered, the shock of penetration too much as she took him in to the hilt. But then he began to move, bumping a place deep inside. The pleasure intensified as she moved with him, taking him deeper still in a wild, unstoppable ride to oblivion.

The orgasm hit hard, in a wave that went on and on until it crested with the speed and force of a tsunami. Slamming into her, robbing her of breath, it powered through from the tips of her toes to the top of her head. She heard his shout of completion, the sound a million miles away as her body shattered into glittery shards of ecstasy.

She collapsed on top of him, his sweat-slicked body slippery against her own.

His hands stroked her buttocks, roamed up her back. 'I never thought I'd say this, but that was actually worth the wait.'

An exhausted grin formed on her lips as she settled beside him, and he tucked her under his arm. She rested her hand on his chest, stroked down the elegant line of hair, and her fingertips touched the raised edge of the scar that slashed across his abdomen. The grin died as tenderness engulfed her, and her heart careered into her ribcage.

Foolish tears prickled the backs of her eyelids. She blinked furiously, struggling to find something witty and clever to say to push the emotion back where it belonged.

Their love-making had been wild and uncontrolled. It had felt like more than just sex. But how much more? And why did the thought suddenly terrify her?

He tipped her face up to his. 'You okay? I was a little rough.'

'No, you weren't, I enjoyed it,' she said, her cheeks flushing at the smile that curved his lips.

Well, it wasn't exactly witty or clever, but at least it was accurate.

His thumb trailed down her cheek as he studied her face, his golden gaze still dazed with afterglow. 'So did I.' The soft words had her heart jumping into her throat again.

She traced the line of the scar and felt him tense. 'How did you get this scar?'

Sadness overwhelmed her when she watched the haze of arousal clear from his eyes and the familiar caution return.

Taking his arm from around her, he sat up with his back to her. She noticed the stiff set of his shoulders as he dragged his T-shirt over his head, covering the scar.

'We should head back,' he said, as if she hadn't said anything, then grabbed his boxers up and stood to put them on. 'Before they come looking for us.'

She reached for a bed sheet to cover herself, acutely aware of her own nakedness, and swallowed down the stupid lump of hurt at the way he had ignored her question. What they had wasn't permanent and her curiosity was just that. Curiosity. If he didn't feel comfortable talking about his past, he certainly didn't have to.

'Do you think the duca will guess what we've been doing?'

she asked, concerned about what the old man might make of their behaviour. She doubted he'd be all that impressed.

'Maybe.' He shrugged, glancing over his shoulder while fastening the button-fly of his jeans. 'But who cares? I expect Eduardo will inform him we're sharing a bedroom before too long.'

She shot upright, clutching the bed sheet to her bosom. 'We can't share a bedroom.'

'Yeah, we can,' he said easily. 'And we will.'

'But…Then everyone will know,' she said, worrying her bottom lip. 'Maybe we could just—'

'Eva, sweetheart,' he interrupted her panicked reasoning, sitting down on the edge of the bed. 'As much as I enjoy playing pirate captain to your damsel in distress—' he tucked a strand of hair behind her ear '—no way in hell am I risking my neck on that balcony every night to have you.'

She let out a jerky breath, the tenderness of his touch making the foolish emotion rush back. 'But you don't have to. We have the connecting bathroom. You could easily—'

'No, I couldn't.' He silenced her with a quick kiss. 'I'm not sneaking around like some horny teenager. I want you in my bed at night.' He gave his eyebrows a saucy lift. 'And in the morning—and any other time in between that takes our fancy. We've got another week and a half here and I plan to have you as much as is humanly possible. If you don't want me, all you have to do is say so.'

'I *do* want you,' she said. 'You know I do.'

But did she want him too much?

They only had a week and a half, and she had to keep sight of that. She mustn't let her romantic nature and her affection for him—not to mention their thrilling sexual chemistry—get in the way of her common sense.

But she could take that risk, she decided. She was ready—and she was through being a coward about her own needs and desires.

'Well, good.' His smile turned to a triumphant grin. He grasped her waist and tumbled her back onto the bed. 'But you'd better get dressed pronto,' he added. She shrieked, giddy with excitement, as he wrestled the sheet off to nuzzle her exposed nipple.

'Or I'm going to make you prove it.'

And then he did.

CHAPTER SIXTEEN

'THERE you are. What are you hiding in here for?'

Eva looked up from the exquisite parchment that had the Alegria family tree hand-drawn on it by fourteenth-century monks, to see Nick striding into the palazzo's library with a frown on his face and a picnic basket under his arm.

'Studying your ancestors,' she replied, acknowledging the flutter of excitement that always gripped her when she saw him again.

'Don't start. I've already had a lecture about my so-called ancestors from Don Vincenzo today,' he said, but to her joy he sounded exasperated rather than upset.

It had been over a week since she'd eavesdropped on his lunch with Don Vincenzo—and since then she'd enjoyed watching his relationship with his grandfather soften and grow. She knew Nick was still opposed to inheriting the palazzo, but Don Vincenzo had proved to be patient and kind and surprisingly astute—and he'd worn down Nick's resistance to him on every other front. The two men had a lot in common, despite Nick's attempts to dwell on their differences, and it had been sweet to see him struggling to cope with his growing affection for the old man. She wondered if he knew he was making an attachment here he would find it hard to break.

'I thought you had a whole day of meetings with Don

Vincenzo's lawyers in Milan?' she said, inordinately pleased to see him back so soon.

'Not any more.' Grabbing her wrist, he hauled her out of the chair. 'I gave them the slip,' he said, dragging her out of the room and down the corridor. 'We're playing hooky for the rest of the day.'

'We are?' she asked, excitement making her voice rise.

He squeezed her hand and grinned. 'Yeah, we are.' He lifted the wicket basket. 'And I've bought supplies so we don't have to come back till we start to starve.'

She giggled, like a child escaping from the classroom, as he led her out of the palazzo's back door, then climbed the steeply terraced ornamental gardens towards an overgrown orchard of lemon trees. As they trekked down the country lane through the trees Eva struggled to keep pace with his long strides and control the ecstatic flutter of her heartbeat at the promise of a new adventure.

She'd become addicted to the adrenaline rush of being Nick Delisantro's lover. Their time together had rushed past in a haze of hot passion-filled nights and long lazy days as they explored Lake Garda and its surrounding towns and villages—and every inch of each other's bodies. He never ceased to surprise her, to arouse her, to provoke and excite her—and she'd found herself conquering every challenge and rejoicing in every risk.

In fact, she was a little bit afraid she might have become as wild as he was. But she couldn't seem to find the will to worry about it too much. And if there were moments when she held him a little too tightly, when she had to bite back the urge to ask him to confide more about himself and the demons that she knew still haunted him, or wondered about how she was going to cope back in her old life when their time was up, she refused to dwell on them. This was a once-in-a-lifetime adventure that had already changed her for ever. She'd become so much bolder, so much more independent and she was loving the new, improved, devil-may-care Eva Redmond far too much to force her back into her shell even when her dangerous lover was no longer by her side to tempt her into trouble.

And she didn't need to know about Nick's past, because she'd already come to terms with the fact that they had no future together. There were only two days left until he returned to San Francisco and she went back to London. And while neither of them had mentioned it, they both knew it was coming.

Eventually they reached a sloping meadow, a good mile above the palazzo, edged by ancient trees, and carpeted with wild flowers. She toed off her sandals and let her bare toes sink into the course grass and fragrant blooms. A light breeze tempered the scorching heat of the summer sun.

Dumping the basket on the ground, Nick flopped down on his back beside it. 'We're stopping here,' he said, hooking his hands behind his head. 'That thing weighs a bloody ton.'

Eva laughed. 'Fine by me, Romeo,' she teased.

'Hey, don't get cocky. I wheedled lunch out of Maria, didn't I?' he grumbled, mentioning the palazzo's chef, just one of the many members of staff who Eva knew adored him—so she doubted much wheedling had been involved. 'And hefted it all the way up here,' he finished.

'Fair enough.' She grinned, kneeling next to him to open the basket. 'I'll carry it back.'

'Big deal,' he said, lifting up on an elbow to pluck out a chilled bottle of Pinot Grigio, while Eva laid out the checkered cloth Maria had packed. 'It'll be empty by then.'

She snorted out an unladylike laugh at the disgruntled expression on his face as she laid out the array of mouthwatering anti-pasti dishes.

Finding a corkscrew, he twisted it into the bottle in a few efficient strokes and yanked the cork with a satisfying pop. 'Laugh all you want, sweetheart, but I intend to exact a high price for all my hard work.'

He handed her a chilled glass of the pale amber wine.

'Oh, goodie!' she said cheekily, enjoying the way his eyes darkened dangerously as she took a fortifying sip.

Nick watched Eva eat as he devoured his meal—and thought about devouring her. The agonising sexual tension tightened deliciously every time she flicked him a flirtatious glance over the rim of her wine glass, or when she tore open a ripe fig and bit into the succulent fruit or licked the sweet juice off her lips.

God, she was so gorgeous. So lush and sexy and playful and provocative. She turned him on to the point of madness, simply by breathing. And yet she'd proved to be a surprisingly calming influence when it came to dealing with all the tangled emotions that the time he spent with his grandfather seemed to bring to the surface.

Even on that day over a week ago, when he'd overreacted so spectacularly to Don Vincenzo's decision to leave his estate to him, having her on the boat beside him, being able to lose himself in her had been enough to take the turmoil and the anger away.

He still didn't want the damn inheritance, not that Don Vincenzo would listen to any of his objections, but he didn't feel nearly so trapped now, so scared of accepting the old man's affection. And the main reason for that had been Eva's presence. He didn't know how or why. But he did know he was going to miss her when he had to go back to San Francisco alone—her bright sense of humour, her easy affection, even her foolish concern for his feelings about this reunion or her misplaced faith in his integrity, not to mention her sexy, responsive little body. She made him feel lighter and more carefree than he had since he was a boy.

He hurled the hunk of ciabatta he'd been eating into the underbrush. No need to worry about their parting yet, he still had another couple of days to enjoy her. Brushing his hands on his hiking shorts, he crooked a finger at her. 'Picnic's over, sweetheart. It's payback time.'

Putting down her paper plate slowly, she darted a glance to her right. 'Only if you catch me first,' she said, then, to his amazement, leapt onto her feet in one fluid movement and shot off like a gazelle.

He swore and levered himself up to chase after her. She was a lot faster than he would have given her credit for, plus he had a belly full of food to contend with. So they were both breathless and laughing hard when he finally tagged her round the waist and slung her to the ground, rolling over to take the brunt of the fall and then settling on top of her.

Holding her wrists in one hand, he levered them above her head and looked down into her laughing eyes as she wriggled furiously trying to buck him off. 'So finally I know how you stayed a virgin so long,' he joked. 'You run faster than an Olympic sprinter.'

Her body stilled and she looked away, the flags of colour on her cheeks flying high.

'Hey, I'm kidding,' he said. He'd embarrassed her and he hadn't meant to.

She looked back. 'That's okay.'

'No, it's not. Tell me what's wrong.'

'It's nothing,' she said, but the vivid colour on her cheeks said otherwise.

He let go of her wrists, but kept her pinned to the ground. 'It's not nothing. What did I say?'

He saw her swallow, knew that shuttered look that meant she was building up the courage to ask something. 'Does it still bother you? That I was a virgin?'

He wanted to laugh off the question. Say of course it didn't bother him. But the problem was it did. Now more than ever. Because however hard he'd tried he couldn't explain away the feeling of responsibility towards her that kept growing every time they made love. Every time she clung to him and begged him for release. Every time she sobbed out his name while reaching orgasm. Every time he taught her a new way to please him, or showed her a new way he could please her. The truth was he loved knowing he was the first man who had ever made her feel that way—and apart from making him feel like a Neanderthal jerk, it scared the hell out of him, because it made no sense at all. He didn't have any claim on her, any more than she did on him, and he didn't want to have, so why did he feel so possessive?

'Fine.' He forced a self-deprecating smile to his lips. 'It does bother me a bit.' His hands settled on her waist, the thin satin of her dress brushing his palms. 'I want to know why it took you so long.'

'If I tell you,' she began, her hands covering his, her eyes thoughtful, 'would you tell me something about yourself in return?'

Damn, he should have seen that one coming. But instead of evading her, as he had always done before, he nodded. 'It's a deal.' Holding her hands, he leant forward and kissed the warm sun-kissed skin on the tip of her nose. 'So what's your answer?'

'You have to promise not to laugh,' she added, colouring again, and looking so vulnerable his heart lurched in his chest.

'I won't laugh,' he said, and he knew he wouldn't. Whatever reasons she had for denying the passion inside her for so long, he had a feeling he wasn't going to like them.

'Can I sit up?'

He wanted to say no, but could see she needed the distance. 'All right.' He lifted off her.

Hugging her knees to her chest, she looked out into the meadow at the afternoon sun dipping towards the trees. 'Actually it's remarkably boring,' she said carefully. 'I didn't do much socialising when I was a teenager.'

'Why not?'

She jerked her shoulder looking surprised at the question.

Although he didn't know why she would be. She was such a lively, engaging person.

'I was horribly nerdy. My parents were academics and they wanted me to concentrate on my studies. And I wanted to please them.'

She made it sound simple. But he wasn't convinced. Why had she been so dead set on pleasing them?

'By the time I got to university I was two years ahead of my peers. And I didn't know the first thing about boys.' She gave a hopeless little laugh. 'Plus I think my love of pirate fantasies may have given me some unrealistic expectations. And by the time I got over that, and realised that swashbuckling sex gods are quite thin on the ground in real life, I was stuck in such a huge rut it took someone spectacular to kick me out of it.'

The shy smile she sent him had his heart tripping over. He skimmed his thumb down her cheek. 'Please tell me you don't mean me.'

No one had ever thought he was spectacular before. And he knew he wasn't. So why did it feel so good to hear her say it?

She wiggled her eyebrows suggestively. 'Only in a sexual sense, you understand.'

'You little tease,' he said softly, framing her face. Then he kissed her.

Her lips softened, and he fed on the sweet, heady taste of figs and innocence. The soft sigh that issued against his cheek made it hard to focus. But he forced himself to draw back. Not to take her in the quick greedy gulps he wanted to.

'It's kind of ironic, don't you think?' he said, trying to lighten the mood and dispel the feeling of hopelessness that threatened to engulf him. 'That you were a good girl and did what your parents wanted, while I was a rebel and did the opposite. And yet we both ended up regretting it.'

Her eyes flickered with something that looked like sadness. 'Why *did* you run away from home?'

The sixty-four-thousand-dollar question, he thought grimly.

'Was that your question?' he asked, stalling.

She nodded. He debated giving her a sanitised version. Or making something up that would deflect her from the truth about who he really was. It wouldn't be the first time he'd lied to a woman after all.

But as he met her trusting gaze he knew he couldn't lie to her. Better to take the stars out of her eyes, once and for all.

'When my dad came home from the hospital the night Mum died, I was fourteen,' he began, the horror of that long ago summer night making his gut churn. 'I thought my whole world had collapsed. But it hadn't. Not yet.'

Eva could hear the tension in his voice, see the rigid control in his face and wanted desperately to take the pain away he was trying so hard to hide.

She touched his arm. 'It's okay, Nick. You don't have to tell me.'

'Yeah, I do,' he said, the tone gruff. 'My dad was wild with grief. She'd told him the truth. That I wasn't his biological son. And he lost it for a while.'

Tears pricked her eyes. She hated to think what that meant—and how deeply he had been hurt by an incident that even now he couldn't bring himself to describe.

'He apologised a few days later at her funeral,' Nick continued, plucking a tuft of grass, flinging it away. 'He said it didn't matter. That he still loved me, still considered me to be his son. But I wouldn't believe him.'

Eva sniffed, scrubbed away the tears.

Nick's head shot up and he scowled. 'Don't you dare cry, Eva. Not for me.'

'Why not? It must have been dreadful for you.'

'It wasn't that bad,' he said, as if the trauma he had suffered that night had been nothing at all. When she knew how bad it must have been, if he was unable to acknowledge the pain, even now.

'I made him pay for that lapse for the rest of his life,' he said grimly. 'Him and my sister Ruby. I made their lives hell for two years.' He thrust his fingers through his hair, the gesture defensive and full of frustration. 'I got into fights, bunked off school, argued with him constantly. And then I ran off and got up to much worse on the streets. And I didn't go back. Ever. Even when Ruby begged me to. Even when he was dying.'

The loathing in his voice was so intense, so bitter, she didn't know how to get past it. 'You mustn't blame yourself,' she said, the tears flowing freely now. 'You were a frightened, confused child.'

'You think?' he said, the cynicism brutal and unyielding—and nothing like the warm, wonderful man she had discovered in the last two weeks. 'I know what I'm capable of,' he added, his lips twisting in a bitter smile. 'I've known it ever since I was a kid. And now I've read Leonardo's journal, I know why.'

Standing up, he walked back to the picnic basket.

She ran after him, pulled him round to face her. 'You're wrong. You're nothing like Leonardo,' she blurted out, knowing it was true, wanting to make him believe it, but not knowing how.

He shook his head, his expression closed off and unreadable, deliberately shutting her out. 'How would you know?' was all he said—and her newfound courage deserted her.

Kicking the lid of the basket closed, he shoved it under his arm and glanced at the grey clouds that had covered the sun. 'We better get back to the palazzo—it's going to rain.'

She looped her arm through his as they walked back, but she could already feel him slipping away. And felt powerless to do anything about it—the fresh citrus scent of the lemon orchard a cruel reminder of the short-lived new Eva.

He made love to her that night, bringing her to orgasm countless times, and taking his own pleasure with ruthless efficiency, the seduction brutal and relentless as if to prove that sex was all he had ever wanted—until she fell into an exhausted sleep.

She woke groggy and sore the next morning to find him gone—and opened the note sitting on the dresser with trembling fingers.

Stay sweet, Eva. And go find one of the good guys.

And then she sobbed as if her foolish romantic heart were shattering.

Because it was.

CHAPTER SEVENTEEN

'HEY, what's the matter, man? Something wrong with the beer?'

Nick tuned out the comment from his publicist Jay, his gaze locked on the tall, willowy blonde standing on the other side of the art gallery. He'd recognised her as soon as she'd walked in a minute ago.

Eva's friend, Tess…Something. He'd been to three different openings at this godforsaken gallery in the last six weeks, ever since he'd returned to San Francisco, and he had never admitted to himself the reason why he kept coming back here.

But the miserable truth was suddenly staring him in the face with startling clarity. Because as soon as Eva's friend had appeared, his heartbeat had rocketed into his throat—just as it did every night when he struggled to fall asleep in his empty bed, or when he switched on his computer only to spend the rest of the day staring at a blank screen.

He hadn't got over Eva. Hadn't been able to forget her. Because even the most tenuous link to her made him feel like crap.

'Hey, Earth to Nick,' Jay said, swinging his palm in front of Nick's eyes.

Nick passed the lukewarm beer to his publicist. 'Hold this,' he said, ignoring Jay's puzzled frown as he headed through the crowd.

Sweat popped out on his forehead and made his hands feel clammy. He ignored it.

This wasn't a big deal. He wasn't going to make it a big deal. Maybe all he really needed was closure? Something he'd denied himself by not saying goodbye to Eva properly. And here was the perfect opportunity. He could have a quick chat with Eva's friend, just to see how Eva was doing. And then he'd finally be able to stop thinking about her. Every damn second, of every damn day. And every damn night.

He'd waited patiently for her to contact him. To ask him to come back. But it had been six weeks, and she hadn't. So he had to let it go now.

As he approached the woman he formulated the best way to introduce himself casually in case she didn't remember him. But then she lifted her head, laughing at something her friend had said, and spotted him.

The laugh died on her lips and her eyes narrowed sharply as he stopped in front of her.

'Well, if it isn't the playboy screenwriter,' she said.

He frowned at the outright hostility in her tone. Seemed she remembered him all right. 'The name's Nick.'

'I know your name.' She flicked a derisive glance over him that had his temper prickling. 'Although I can think of several other names which would suit you better.'

'Have you got a problem with me?' To hell with polite introductions. He'd hardly slept in close to two months, his writing had been shot to hell, and now he was getting the third degree from someone he barely knew. What was up with that?

She glared back. 'You treated the kindest, sweetest, most genuine woman I know as your personal plaything. Then dumped her like she was nothing. So yes, we do have a problem.'

'What are you talking about?' His voice cracked, the shock at her attack nothing compared to the emotion banding around his chest.

That wasn't the way it had happened at all. He'd done the decent thing. He'd had no claim on Eva and very little to offer her. So he'd walked away. And left it up to her. Even though it had nearly killed him. Was still killing him. He deserved a damn medal.

'Don't you get it?' She fired the words at him. 'You destroyed her, you creep. She cried over you for weeks. And she never cries.' The girl's diatribe washed over him as temper gave way to regret and confusion. If she'd felt that much for him, why hadn't she contacted him?

He'd given her a choice. Why hadn't she taken it?

'But the good news is,' the girl continued, her eyes boring into him, 'she's over you now. She's met a great guy. And he treats her right.'

The hell she had. The temper he'd been trying to muster came surging back to life.

'What guy? What's his name?' He'd strangle the bastard.

She couldn't have got over him so easily—not when he wasn't over her.

'It's…' The girl hesitated. 'It's Bill and he's a…' Another slight pause. 'A computer programmer.'

A computer programmer called Bill! What the…?

No way. Eva wouldn't be happy with someone like that. She needed adventure. She needed passion and excitement in her life. She was like a beautiful flower burst into bloom. And she'd damn well bloomed with him. Which meant she didn't get to bloom with anyone else.

'The hell with that,' he snarled under his breath. Then turned and walked out of the art gallery, the emotion burning his throat bursting into flames.

So she thought she could just take up with someone else? *I don't think so.*

It wasn't over. Not till he said so. He'd done the decent thing and given her a damn choice. And she'd thrown it back in his face. He still wanted her. And he needed her. And she needed him. Not some computer nerd called Bill. End of story.

Hailing a cab, Nick shouted at the driver as he launched himself into the back seat. 'Take me to the airport. I've got a plane to catch.'

He'd been through six long weeks of torture and now she thought she could just blow him off. Well, she could forget it. He was through hanging around. And he was through pretending to be a nice guy.

'Eva, it's me, Tess. We need to talk.'

'Tess?' Eva glanced at the clock on her computer—just past two o'clock in the afternoon London time on a Saturday afternoon. 'Is everything all right?' Why was Tess calling so early in the morning? She never got up before noon on a weekend.

'Everything's wonderful,' Tess's voice came down the phone line, but she didn't sound too sure.

'Okay,' Eva said carefully. Tess could be a bit of a drama queen, but she sounded genuinely worried. 'So what do we need to talk about?'

'I did something a tiny bit rash last night. And I thought I should let you know.' There was a long pause. 'In case there are consequences.'

'Consequences?' That didn't sound good. 'What did you do?'

'I bumped into Nick Delisantro at the Union Square gallery.'

'Oh.' Eva felt the sharp tug of grief at the mention of his name, and hated herself for it. 'I see' she said dully, forcing the words out.

She was over him. She had to be. It had been over a month and a half since she'd woken up in the master suite in the palazzo to find him gone. And she'd changed beyond all recognition from that devastated woman who had cried herself hoarse for two solid weeks, until she was hollowed out and exhausted and simply had no tears left in her.

Admittedly, it had taken her even longer to call a halt to her pity party and put her wild fling with Nick Delisantro into its proper perspective.

Yes she'd fallen for him. Hard and fast and far too easily. And once she'd finally got past the howling grief of losing him, it had been pathetically obvious to figure out why.

In his own way, Nick Delisantro had been everything she'd always fantasised about in her dream man. Tough and untamed, unconventional and wildly exciting on the outside but surprisingly tender and thoughtful and troubled on the inside. He'd made her feel beautiful and exciting and vivid. He'd lifted her life out of the ordinary and made it extraordinary. And most of all he'd made her feel important. The way her parents never had.

But it wasn't until she'd received an email from Don Vincenzo a little over a month ago that she'd realised the bold, exciting person she had believed herself to be with Nick was as much of a fraud as the timid, mouse-like person she had been before she met him.

The duca had been as devastated as she was to find Nick gone that morning without a word. But unlike her, he hadn't been willing to simply accept Nick's departure. According to the email the duca had sent her a fortnight later, Nick had refused to acknowledge his many attempts to contact him and Eva could tell that had devastated the elderly man. But the duca had finished by thanking her for her part in his reunion with his grandson and stating that he hadn't given up hope—assuring her that however stubborn Nick was, the Duca D'Alegria was more so.

Eva hadn't doubted the old man for a moment, and as she'd read the email at her cluttered desk in Roots Registry she'd felt the first stirrings of something other than misery.

A fragile glimmer of hope had peeped through the fog of

despair and then she'd had a devastating moment of enlightenment. Nick wasn't responsible for her courage, or her lack of it. She was. He couldn't give her the guts to be herself. To be the bright, bold, confident woman she'd always wanted to be. Only she could do that. And even though she couldn't make Nick Delisantro love her or make him accept the love she had for him in return, she could still be that woman.

And so she'd walked into Henry Crenshawe's office that afternoon and handed in her notice.

The next month had flown past as she'd pushed her broken heart to the back of her mind and concentrated all her efforts on remaking herself into the real Eva Redmond. She'd chucked out her wardrobe full of biege. She'd got a business loan, moved out of her dull suburban semi, moved into a chic little studio flat in Stoke Newington, and launched her own web-based heir-hunting and ancestral research business. Her client list was still small, but, with her overheads minimal and the two big contracts she'd secured from her contacts at Roots Registry, she had made an excellent start.

The only big blot on her horizon had been her complete inability to start dating. Which she had a terrible feeling derived from some subconscious belief that she'd never be able to find anyone to replace Nick.

She clutched the phone tighter, forcing back the urge to slam it down.

'How is he?' she heard herself ask Tess.

She could do this. She could have a conversation about him without bursting into tears. She had to. If she was ever going to be free of him for good.

'Really angry actually,' came Tess's reply.

'Angry with whom?' Eva said, curiosity going some way to dim the pain.

'With you.'

Eva's eyes popped wide. 'Why would he be angry with me?'

'It has to do with Bill, the computer programmer.'

'Bill? Bill who? I don't know anyone called Bill,' Eva said, not just curious now but completely confused.

'Bill's… Well, Bill's a long story.' Tess's voice rose, getting more dramatic by the second. 'And he's sort of beside the point,' she added evasively. 'The thing is, I saw Nick. And he was looking all sexy and intense and gorgeous. And then he came up to me. I think to ask about you. And I got so angry with him I totally lost it and stupidly told him how devastated you were when he dumped you.'

'Oh, Tess, you didn't.' The thought of Nick knowing about the extent of her meltdown had humiliation stabbing under her breastbone right alongside the pain. In those dark days after his departure, the one thing she'd had was her pride. She could always feel relieved that she'd never blurted out the truth to him and told him how hard she'd fallen for him.

And now she didn't have that any more.

'But listen,' her friend began. 'There is a good side to this. Because, Eva, from his reaction, I'm totally convinced he's not over you. Honestly, he went pale. And then he got all fired up when I told him about Bill. He stormed out of the gallery.' Tess huffed out a deep breath, the frantic tumble of information stuttering to a halt. 'I think he might be coming to London. To see you.'

Eva squeezed her eyes shut, let the wave of misery wash through her.

Nick wasn't coming to see her. Why would he? If he'd wanted to be with her, he never would have left her the way he had. Or at the very least he would have contacted her long before now. Tess with her overactive imagination and gung-ho personality had simply misinterpreted his reaction and read into it the most ridiculous scenario possible.

'Look, Tess. Thanks for letting me know.' She drew in a steadying breath. 'But don't worry, I'm sure nothing will come of it.'

She ended the call as quickly as possible and settled the phone back in its cradle. Then took a deep breath.

Stop that right now.

She wasn't going to let herself get sucked under again. She was a stronger person now. A more confident, more independent, much less fragile person. Who was not going to get all choked up about a guy who had always been wrong for her.

Pushing away from the desk, she made her way to the hall closet and pulled on her raincoat. That said, she might as well admit that after Tess's call she was unlikely to get any more work done today. She'd go for a walk to Clissold Park. The new café there was always buzzing with people and the chilly autumn air would do her good and stop her moping around the flat, thinking about things—and people—it would be better for her not to think about.

The brisk wind ruffled her hair as she stepped out onto the pavement and locked the door behind her. She noticed the taxi stopped at the kerb in front of the house, just as a tall, painfully familiar figure got out.

'Eva?'

Shock came first, before the tumult of emotions she'd thought she'd conquered surged back up her torso.

'What are you doing here?' Her voice echoed from a million miles away.

'I want you back.'

She stared at him. That sharply handsome face that had haunted her dreams. And knew she couldn't do this. She wasn't ready.

She had a good life. It wasn't safe and secure any more. Thank goodness. Now she had challenges. Now she was her own person. Now she was the real Eva Redmond who had guts and courage galore. But he could take all that away from her… If she let him.

'Don't…' She shook her head fiercely. 'I can't.'

Ignoring the look of confusion on his face, she turned and ran.

'Eva, wait! Damn it. Come back here!' Nick shouted, his voice raw.

He'd been riveted to the spot by the unexpected sight of her walking out of the building. She'd lost weight, and her eyes, those luminous blue eyes, had lost the trusting look he remembered. But then he registered the sound of her feet pounding on the pavement and he sprinted after her.

He caught her in a few strides, grabbed her round the waist and hauled her back against him.

'Let go of me.' She stiffened, struggled, tried to prise his arms from around her waist. 'I can't do this. Go away.'

He inhaled, smelt the glorious scent of spring flowers in her hair, and held her tight, the slope of her breasts warm against his forearm. 'We have to talk.'

She bristled, her fingers digging into his forearms. 'You have to let me go,' she said. 'I don't want to talk to you.'

He lowered her feet back to the floor, released his arms, and she spun round to face him.

'I don't want you back,' she said, but her voice trembled and he saw the flicker of uncertainty in her eyes. She was lying. He knew she was. She still wanted him. His heart stopped kicking his ribcage and swelled into his throat.

Grasping her hand, he squeezed hard, the euphoria of having her close again overwhelming him. 'Yes, you do,' he murmured, already anticipating the reunion he'd been obsessing about during the long, sleepless night flight from San Francisco. 'Dump Bill.'

She yanked her hand out of his. 'There isn't any Bill. Tess made him up.'

'Huh?'

'You heard me. I don't have a boyfriend. But I don't need one to know I'm not going to fall for you again.' Her eyes sparkled with temper, making the dark blue turn to a vivid violet. She looked indomitable and wilful and more beautiful than even he could remember, and he remembered a lot. But he had no clue what she was talking about.

'Fall for me?'

'Oh, come on, Nick. Let's not be coy.' She thrust her chin out in a gesture he did remember, but this time there wasn't an ounce of hesitation about it. 'You know perfectly well I fell hopelessly in love with you. That's why you turned tail and ran.'

He'd heard the declaration before, from other women, delivered in clinging, dulcet tones, or in simpering desperation. Tons of times. And it had never meant anything to him. He'd never once heard it delivered like a slap, with the spark and sizzle of anger and indignation and the underlying tone of misery. And this time it meant everything.

But instead of taking her declaration and trying to make himself believe it, he said, 'You don't love me—you can't,' in automatic defence. However happy he was to see Eva again. However much he'd missed her. However much he might want her back. He would never ask for that. Would never expect it. Especially not from her. Not when he would only hurt her. The way he'd hurt everyone else who mattered.

'Don't tell me how I feel.' She hurled the words at him. The moment of fragility he'd witnessed disappearing as quickly as it had come. 'You arrogant…' she sputtered. 'You egotistical…'

'Berk?' he offered.

Her eyes narrowed, but not before he saw the unshed tears. 'Yes, berk,' she said, the anger subsiding to be replaced by something much more disturbing. 'You broke my heart, Nick, when you dumped me, but I've spent the last six weeks healing.' She hitched a shaky breath into her lungs, and the bottom dropped out of his stomach. 'And maybe I haven't healed all the way, yet. But I will.' She shoved her hair back behind her ear, her fingers trembling slightly. 'Goodbye.'

She turned her back on him, started to walk away.

'I didn't dump you,' he said, his voice hoarse, but the words surprisingly clear despite the swish of passing traffic on the rain-slick streets. 'That's not how it was. I left to protect you.'

Eva stopped dead at the low words, turned round. 'To protect me from *what* exactly?' she asked. Did he really think she was going to believe that?

'From me,' he replied, frustration edging the words. 'What the hell do you think?'

Her eyebrows shot up her forehead. 'You're not serious!' She could see it in his eyes, the shuttered, defensive look making her heartbeat stumble. But as much as she wanted to give in to the tenderness, to hold him close and tell him he was mad to think so little of himself, more than that she felt anger. At what he'd put her through. At what he'd put them both through. With his stupid inability to accept the truth about who he really was.

She marched back to him and socked him hard in the chest. 'You stupid berk!' she shouted, having no difficulty whatso-ever remembering the name this time.

He stumbled back, his eyes widening. 'What was that for?'

'I cried for weeks after you left me that stupid note. And now you're telling me you did it for my own good.' The more she thought about it, the more she wanted to hit him again. 'Like I was a silly immature little girl who couldn't make up my own mind about who to love…'

'You were a virgin, damn it,' he shouted back, rubbing his chest where she'd punched him and looking aggrieved. 'How could you know you loved me? When you'd never been with anyone *but* me.'

She waved her hand, her temper growing and intensifying like a living thing. 'Oh, for pity's sake, will you please just get over that now? I'm not a virgin any more.' And then she remembered the wording of his note. The note that she'd mooned over and soaked with her own tears for weeks, and her temper ignited. 'That's what it meant.' She fired the words like bullets, glad when he flinched. 'That crass line about me finding one of the good guys. You wanted me to sleep around. Because until I do I can't possibly have the emotional maturity to know how I feel—is that it?'

'What?' He looked horrified, his face going bloodless beneath his tan. 'I *did not* tell you to sleep around.'

'Didn't you?' She slapped her hands on her hips, warming to her theme. 'Tell me something, Nick. Exactly how many guys do I have to sleep with before I can be trusted to decide for myself who I love?' She poked a finger into the middle of his chest. Hard. 'You should probably give me a number, so I can be absolutely sure.'

He grabbed her finger, pulled her close. 'Forget it. You're not sleeping with anyone but me,' he yelled back, his own temper rising to match hers. 'I gave you the choice and you fell for me anyway. You said so.' He wrapped his arm round her waist, pulled her flush against him. 'So now you're stuck with me.'

Her heart soared at the angry words, and heat pulsed low in her abdomen. This was what she'd dreamed of after he'd left her. That he'd come back. That he'd stake a claim, make a declaration, and finally get past that warped sense of honour that had made him believe he wasn't good enough for her.

But even as euphoria rushed through her, she refused to give in to the heady thrill. She struggled out of his arms, stepped back. What he offered wasn't enough. And the new powerful, risk-taking Eva Redmond wasn't willing to settle for second best any more. She didn't just want the dream. She wanted the reality—but that meant risking everything.

'You walked away from me, Nick,' she said, her voice low.

'You didn't give me a choice. You didn't tell me how you felt. You didn't give me the chance to tell you how I felt. You simply made the choice for me.' She blinked back the threatening tears. She had to do it. For his sake as well as her own.

'That's not true, I—'

She pressed a finger to his lips, to cut off the denial. 'What if Tess hadn't told you I had a new boyfriend, Nick? Would you have come here? Or would you have let me keep on waiting?'

She didn't need to hear his answer, she could see it in his face. See it in the way he stiffened and thrust his fists into the pockets of his jeans. 'I wanted to leave it up to you,' he muttered.

She shook her head. 'You ran away, Nick. Just like you've been doing all your life. When things get hard, when things get scary or complicated. When you can't control the way you feel. That's what you do, you run away.' She sniffed, scrubbed away a solitary tear.

'I *do* love you.' She cupped his cheek, felt the rasp of his stubble and the muscle in his jaw tighten and knew that however much she'd tried to deny it, that would always be true.

'I love the dangerous, wild and exciting man you are in bed and out. And the kind, tender and stupidly noble man you don't even know is there. And I feel nothing but sorrow for the boy you were. Who discovered something devastating about himself at the most difficult moment imaginable, and couldn't cope.' She let her hand slip away from his face. 'But I don't want another fling. I want to make a life with you. And I can't do that unless you love me back enough to finally let that boy go and stop running.'

Her panicked heartbeat flicked in her chest and she swallowed hard, the boulder of emotion in her throat threatening to choke her. She straightened, scared of what he was going to say. Had she pushed him too far? Did he even want to make a life with her? She didn't know. But one thing she did know:

if he ran now, if he rejected her, if she'd asked too much of him, it was better to know. Because she would rather survive the heartache, than live with a lie…

'You've changed,' Nick said, his heart so swollen, he was pretty sure it was about to burst. He couldn't believe she'd offered him everything. Knew he would never deserve it.

She gave a stiff nod, the wry tilt of her lips crucifying him. 'I know. I'm not a doormat any more.'

He choked out a laugh. Then grasped her wrists, hugged her to him. 'You were never a doormat. You were just so…' he searched for the word '…sweet.'

She cringed. 'I'm not sweet. And I don't want to be.'

She was. And she always would be. But he knew that wasn't what she needed to hear.

'The point is, I'm strong.' She looked up at him. 'You don't have to run away, you can just tell me to my face you don't love me. And I'll survive.'

He clasped his arms round her back, and sank his head into her hair to inhale her wonderful scent. 'Yeah, you'll survive.' He hugged her trembling body to his. 'But I sure as hell won't,' he said, wanting to absorb her into him so he would never be without her again. 'I don't just love you, Eva. I'm pretty sure I can't live without you.'

He drew away, held her at arm's length, then saw the smile on her face and took courage from it. 'The last six weeks have been agony. I wanted to contact you countless times, but it was easier to pretend I was being noble, that I was giving you the choice, than admit the truth. That I was scared out of my wits you'd already come to your senses and realised I didn't deserve you.'

'But that's mad, you do deserve—'

He framed her face in his palms, placed a tender kiss on her lips to silence her.

When he pulled back, the stunned pleasure on her face

sent his heart soaring into the stratosphere. 'It doesn't matter any more. Because I'm through running. And I'm going to spend the rest of my life proving that I *do* deserve you.'

She flung her arms round his neck, leaned into his body. 'You really don't have to do that,' she said, sending him a saucy look under her eyelashes that had lust swelling right alongside the joy. 'But if you insist, I know a very good place you can start.'

He threw back his head and laughed—the sheer elation making him light-headed.

Sobering, he let his hands travel down to caress her buttocks through the bulky raincoat, then pulled her against his hardening erection, eager to begin the rest of his life with this sweet, smart and incredibly strong woman by his side.

'That's funny, because so do I,' he murmured.

EPILOGUE

'MAYBE this wasn't such a great idea after all.' Nick stared at the imposing Hampstead mansion block out of the windscreen of the hire car he and Eva had picked up at Heathrow airport an hour ago.

Traffic had been lighter than he'd expected for the day after Boxing Day. Way too light in fact. Was he really ready for this?

Eva's hand settled on his thigh and rubbed gently. 'If you don't want to do this, Nick, you don't have to,' she murmured as if she'd read his mind. 'We can go book into the hotel.' She gave a quiet little laugh. 'From the pictures on their website, the honeymoon suite is amazing.'

Covering her hand, he let go of the breath he'd been holding.

'You booked the honeymoon suite?' He gazed at his wife, and huffed out a laugh, pathetically grateful for her attempt to lighten the mood. 'When we've been married for over six months?'

She wiggled her eyebrows. 'It has the best bed,' she countered, her blue eyes sparking with humour. 'And anyway, they won't know how long we've been married, will they?'

'Really?' He placed his palm on the firm mound of her belly, felt the familiar ripple of love and pride at the thought of the life they'd made together growing inside her. 'This is a bit of a giveaway, don't you think?'

'Not necessarily,' she said laughing. 'We could have been living in sin.' Her brows rose mischievously. 'In fact, we would have been if you hadn't turned out to be such a square,' she finished, a mock pout on her lips.

He chuckled, remembering her initial attempts to persuade him that they didn't *have* to get married just because they'd had a slip-up with their birth control and were becoming parents a lot sooner than planned.

'Sweetheart, give it up...' He curved his hand round her neck to draw her close, touched his nose to hers. 'Your wild days are over.' He nuzzled her lips, letting his hand linger as it caressed the soft hair at her nape. 'I wasn't about to miss the chance to get my ring on your finger. The baby just helped seal the deal.'

Had it really only been two years since she'd agreed to move to San Francisco? She'd changed him so much. Made him a braver, better man than he'd ever thought he could be—making him realise that your life wasn't defined by the mistakes you made, but how you dealt with them.

He'd faced so many of his demons and learned to conquer them with Eva by his side. Best of all, he'd made his peace with Don Vincenzo and the truth about his biological inheritance. With Eva's help, he'd come to accept that he wasn't so much Leonardo's son as Vincenzo's grandson. And getting to know the old man, over the summer months they now spent at the palazzo, and become a part of his family, had given him back the important foundation that he'd lost at sixteen. His lips curved at the memory of Vincenzo's elation when his grandfather had greeted him and Eva as they arrived for Christmas in Lake Garda and spotted her pregnancy.

Nick sighed, and faced the austere mansion block again, where his PA had discovered his sister Ruby now lived with her husband of six years, Callum Westmore. His lips firmed.

The question now was, did he have the guts to finally deal with the biggest mistake of his life?

'Seriously, Nick. You don't have to do this,' Eva said, her voice full of the sweetness and support that had become such an important part of his life.

He looked into her eyes, the smile returning. 'Yeah, I do. It's past time. I want our child to know Ruby.' He rested his palm on Eva's leg. 'I just hope to hell married life has calmed her down a bit, because the kid I remember could create quite a scene when she set her mind to it.'

He climbed out of the car, skirted the bonnet and opened the passenger door for Eva, then slung his arm round her waist. The solid feel of her against his side giving him the courage he needed.

Because the truth was, he'd take a scene any day to what he really feared. That Ruby would cut him dead, the way he deserved.

Eva squeezed Nick's hand as he pressed the buzzer on the mansion's intercom. She could feel the tension vibrating through him, knew how much this meeting meant to him. And while a part of her hoped that Ruby Westmore was a woman with a big heart and a forgiving soul, if she wasn't, Eva already had a contingency plan. No one got to hurt Nick, not even his sister. So the woman would have to go through Eva to do it.

'Who's there?' The high-pitched enquiry crackled out of the panel.

Nick frowned at Eva, clearly as puzzled as she was by the abrupt question. 'Um…We're here to see Ruby Westmore.'

The door buzzed and Nick shoved it open.

They climbed the brightly lit stairwell to the first floor, the building's wrought-iron balustrade and marble flooring matching the gothic frontage. Just as they reached the landing a door opposite the stairwell opened and a little girl standing on a chair peered out. 'My mummy's Ruby Westmore and she's making turkey for dinner. Again,' she announced, her nose wrinkling comically. 'And Daddy's giving Arturo a bath.'

'Oh, I see,' Eva said, when Nick simply stared at the little girl, clearly struggling to process the fact that this stunningly beautiful child with her cap of honey-brown curls and her bright emerald eyes had to be his niece.

'What's your name?' Eva asked.

'My name's Alessia and I'm four and a half. My big brother Max is five and three quarters and he's on a sleepover with his best friend Becca,' she continued without any prompting. 'Daddy says Alessia means trouble in Italian.'

Eva bit into her lip to hold back a grin at the non sequitur. She could just imagine how much trouble.

'It's nice to meet you, Alessia,' she said. 'I'm Eva and this is my husband Nick and we'd really like to talk to one of your parents.'

'Hello,' the girl replied, her gaze dipping to Eva's stomach. 'Do you have a baby in your tummy?' she asked bluntly, happily ignoring the request for parental intervention. 'Mummy had Art in her tummy for ages.' She rolled her eyes and gave a long-suffering sigh worthy of an eighty-year-old. 'But he's out now and Daddy says he's even more trouble than me and Max.'

'Ally, get down off that chair this instant,' a male voice boomed from inside the apartment.

Far from looking worried or even chastened, the little girl shot Eva and Nick an impish grin and whispered loudly from behind her hand, 'That's my daddy.'

The door swung wider and a tall, strikingly handsome man with jet-black hair and the same intense emerald eyes as his daughter stood before them with a cherubic baby haphazardly wrapped in a towel held securely in the crook of his arm.

'Hi, I'm Callum Westmore,' he said tightly, looking harassed with his hair furrowed into rows and a large damp patch on his T-shirt. 'Sorry, I didn't hear the doorbell.'

Before either Eva or Nick could introduce themselves, he turned to his daughter, who had wrapped her arms round his waist from on top of her chair.

'Ally, you little terror,' he said, sounding more exasperated than annoyed. 'How many times have I told you not to answer the door?' he said, his voice softening as he folded his free arm round his daughter's shoulders. 'You're supposed to tell me or Mummy if you hear it ring. Remember?'

The little girl nodded sheepishly, then turned beseeching eyes on her father. 'I forgot, Daddy.'

'I'll just bet you did,' he muttered, but, from the way he was stroking the little girl's shoulders, it was fairly clear he was putty in her hands.

Eva smiled at the tableau Callum Westmore and his children made as he turned his attention back to them. 'Sorry about that. My daughter is like her mother and doesn't follow instructions very well,' he said dryly. 'How can I help you?'

Eva opened her mouth to reply, when Nick answered, his tone stiff. 'I'm Nick Delisantro. We're here to see Ruby. I'm her—'

'I know who you are,' Westmore interrupted sharply, his voice harsh, his brows lowering over eyes that had gone as hard as flint. 'I also know how you treated my wife.' His gaze swept over Nick. 'What makes you think she wants to see you?'

Nick straightened. 'That's between my sister and I.'

Barely restrained violence crackled in the air as the two men squared off across the threshold to the apartment.

Eva placed a restraining hand on Nick's arm, determined to calm the situation down, when little Alessia pointed at her and said happily, apparently oblivious to the tension, 'Look, Daddy, Eva has a baby in her tummy, just like Mummy did.'

Callum Westmore's gaze shifted to Eva and he stared

blankly for several seconds before his gaze lowered to her belly. She realised the exact moment he registered, not just her presence, but her condition as a dull flush appeared on his cheeks. 'I...'

Eva thrust out her hand to rescue him. 'Hello, Mr Westmore, I'm Eva Delisantro, Nick's wife,' she said gently. She might have wanted to dislike the man for his aggressive dislike of Nick, but she couldn't, when it was obvious his anger stemmed from an unflinching loyalty to his wife.

It was also hard not to feel sympathy for his current predicament as she saw him process the fact that he was going to have to back down, with his children looking on and a pregnant lady on his doorstep.

He shook her hand. 'Hello, I didn't mean to—'

'Cal, what's all the commotion? Who's at the door?' a smoky female voice asked before a statuesque beauty appeared beside him.

Eva took in the caramel-coloured curls piled high on the woman's head in a casual knot, the lush, outrageously curvaceous figure that looked stunning even in the simple cotton dress and the captivating chocolate-coloured eyes that went wide with shock as the woman whispered the single word, 'Nick?'

No wonder these two had produced such beautiful children together, Eva thought.

'Hi, Rube,' Nick said, his voice breaking on the nickname. 'I'm here to apologise. For what I did to you and to Dad. Can you forgive me?'

She gave her head a little shake, her lashes dampening with tears. 'Nick,' she murmured again, covering her mouth with her hand. But Eva didn't see anger or derision on her face, all she saw was surprise and an emotion so fierce it was overwhelming.

'Why are you crying, Mummy?' Alessia asked, blunt as ever.

'Ruby, you don't have to do this,' her husband said gently as the baby chortled in his arms. 'I can make him leave if you want me to.'

She glanced at her husband, sending him a spontaneous smile that literally beamed with the love the two of them clearly shared. 'Don't be ridiculous, Cal. He's my brother.'

Then she turned and flung her arms round Nick's neck. 'You idiot,' she said, the joy plain in her voice. 'What the heck took you so long?'

Emotion swelled in Eva's throat and her own eyes filled with tears as she watched Nick wrap his arms round his sister in return.

'Because I was an idiot, obviously,' he replied, wry amusement in his voice as he slanted Eva a smile filled with pleasure and gratitude. 'But I've come to my senses at last.'

'Your sister is a goddess. Her children are adorable and her husband is amazing. You do realize that?' Eva announced as she perched her elbows on her husband's naked chest and peered down at his closed eyes, excitement about what the next day promised making sleep impossible. 'I can't wait to meet Max tomorrow,' she said. 'Although I can't imagine he can be any cuter than Ally,' she continued. 'She certainly took a shine to you,' Eva added, recalling the way the little girl had insisted on sitting on Nick's lap all through supper.

Nick grunted, running a lazy palm down her back. 'Who knew a four-year-old could talk that much?' he said, his lids remaining firmly closed, but she could hear the pleasure in his voice.

The reunion had been an unqualified success, the two couples beginning to form the bonds of a friendship this evening that Eva already knew would last a lifetime.

'Junior's going to get quite a shock,' Eva said, resting a palm on her belly. 'When he meets his cousins.'

She stretched, rubbing seductively against Nick in the honeymoon suite bed, which—despite the gruelling journey from

Italy that day and the emotionally exhausting evening they'd spent with Ruby and her family—they'd managed to give quite a workout.

'Don't you think?' she prompted, tapping her palm on his cheek to get his attention.

His lids lifted to half mast. 'Go to sleep, woman,' he grumbled, his voice thick with exhaustion as he gave her buttocks a firm pat. 'Or I'm going to give you another orgasm to shut you up.'

'Promises promises,' she teased, snuggling against him.

As his breathing deepened into sleep she touched her fingertips to his forehead, pushed the waves of thick caramel hair back from his brow and smiled.

'Guess what, Niccolo Delisantro,' she whispered. 'I found one of the good guys after all.'

* * * * *

COMING NEXT MONTH from Harlequin Presents®
AVAILABLE JULY 31, 2012

#3077 THE SECRETS SHE CARRIED
Lynne Graham

Erin and Christophe's passionate affair ended harshly. Years later, he's bent on revenge, until Erin drops two very important bombshells!

#3078 THE MAN BEHIND THE SCARS
The Santina Crown
Caitlin Crews

Rafe McFarland—Earl of Pembroke and twenty-first-century pinup—has secretly wed tabloid darling Angel in the newest Santina scandal!

#3079 HIS REPUTATION PRECEDES HIM
The Lyonedes Legacy
Carole Mortimer

Eva is hired to decorate Markos Lyonedes's apartment, but the notorious playboy makes it difficult for her to stay out of the bedroom!

#3080 DESERVING OF HIS DIAMONDS?
The Outrageous Sisters
Melanie Milburne

Billionaire Emilio Andreoni needs one thing: the perfect woman. That was once Gisele Carter until headline-grabbing scandals made her the not-so-perfect fiancée!

#3081 THE MAN SHE SHOULDN'T CRAVE
Lucy Ellis

Dating agency owner Rose is in over her head with a new PR proposal involving ruthless Russian ice-hockey team owner Plato Kuragin!

#3082 PLAYING THE GREEK'S GAME
Sharon Kendrick

Few dare to defy global hotel magnate Zac Constantinides—but he's met his match in feisty designer Emma!

REQUEST YOUR FREE BOOKS!

2 FREE NOVELS PLUS
2 FREE GIFTS!

PASSION GUARANTEED SEDUCTION

YES! Please send me 2 FREE Harlequin Presents® novels and my 2 FREE gifts (gifts are worth about $10). After receiving them, if I don't wish to receive any more books, I can return the shipping statement marked "cancel." If I don't cancel, I will receive 6 brand-new novels every month and be billed just $4.30 per book in the U.S. or $4.99 per book in Canada. That's a saving of at least 14% off the cover price! It's quite a bargain! Shipping and handling is just 50¢ per book in the U.S. and 75¢ per book in Canada.* I understand that accepting the 2 free books and gifts places me under no obligation to buy anything. I can always return a shipment and cancel at any time. Even if I never buy another book, the two free books and gifts are mine to keep forever.

106/306 HDN FERQ

Name	(PLEASE PRINT)

Address	Apt. #

City	State/Prov.	Zip/Postal Code

Signature (if under 18, a parent or guardian must sign)

Mail to the **Reader Service:**
IN U.S.A.: P.O. Box 1867, Buffalo, NY 14240-1867
IN CANADA: P.O. Box 609, Fort Erie, Ontario L2A 5X3

Not valid for current subscribers to Harlequin Presents books.

**Are you a current subscriber to Harlequin Presents books
and want to receive the larger-print edition?
Call 1-800-873-8635 or visit www.ReaderService.com.**

* Terms and prices subject to change without notice. Prices do not include applicable taxes. Sales tax applicable in N.Y. Canadian residents will be charged applicable taxes. Offer not valid in Quebec. This offer is limited to one order per household. All orders subject to credit approval. Credit or debit balances in a customer's account(s) may be offset by any other outstanding balance owed by or to the customer. Please allow 4 to 6 weeks for delivery. Offer available while quantities last.

Your Privacy—The Reader Service is committed to protecting your privacy. Our Privacy Policy is available online at www.ReaderService.com or upon request from the Reader Service.

We make a portion of our mailing list available to reputable third parties that offer products we believe may interest you. If you prefer that we not exchange your name with third parties, or if you wish to clarify or modify your communication preferences, please visit us at www.ReaderService.com/consumerchoice or write to us at Reader Service Preference Service, P.O. Box 9062, Buffalo, NY 14269. Include your complete name and address.

HP11B

USA TODAY *bestselling author Lynne Graham brings you a brand-new story of passion and drama.*

THE SECRETS SHE CARRIED

"Don't play games with me," she urged, breathing in deeply and slowly, nostrils flaring in dismay at the familiar spicy scent of his designer aftershave.

The smell of him, so achingly familiar, unleashed a tide of memories. But Cristo had not made a commitment to her, had not done anything to make her feel secure and had never once mentioned love or the future. At the end of the day, in spite of all her precautions, he had still walked away untouched while she had been crushed in the process.

The knowledge that she had meant so little to him that he had ditched her to marry another woman still burned like acid inside her.

"Maybe I'm hoping you'll finally come clean," Cristo murmured levelly.

Erin turned her head, smooth brow indented with a frown as she struggled to recall the conversation and get back into it again. "Come clean about what?"

Cristo pulled off the road into a layby before he responded. "I found out what you were up to while you were working for me at the Mobila spa."

Erin twisted her entire body around to look at him, crystalline eyes flaring bright, her rising tension etched in the taut set of her heart-shaped face. "What do you mean… what I was up to?"

Cristo looked at her levelly, ebony dark eyes cool and opaque as frosted glass. "You were stealing from me."

"I am not a thief," Erin repeated doggedly, although an alarm bell had gone off in her head the instant he mentioned the theft and sale of products from the store.

"I have the proof," Cristo retorted crisply. "You can't talk or charm your way out of this, Erin—"

"I'm not interested in charming you. I'm not the same woman I was when we were together," Erin countered curtly, for what he had done to her had toughened her. There was nothing like surviving an unhappy love affair to build self-knowledge and character, she reckoned painfully. He had broken her heart, taught her how fragile she was, left her bitter and humiliated. But she had had to pick herself up again fast once she'd discovered that she was pregnant.

Cristo is going to make Erin pay back what he believes she stole—in whatever way he demands.... But little does he know that Erin's about to drop two very important bombshells!

Pick up a copy of THE SECRETS SHE CARRIED by Lynne Graham, available August 2012 from Harlequin Presents®.

Harlequin® Super Romance®

*Enjoy a month of compelling, emotional stories, including
a poignant new tale of love lost and found from*

Sarah Mayberry

When Angela Bartlett loses her best friend to a rare heart
condition, it seems only natural that she step in and help
widower and friend Michael Young. The last thing she
expects is to find herself falling for him....

Within Reach

Available August 7!

"I loved it. I thought the story was very believable.
The characters were endearing. The author wrote beautifully...
I will be looking for future books by Sarah Mayberry."

—Sherry, Harlequin® Superromance® reader, on *Her Best Friend*

Find more great stories this month from
Harlequin® Superromance® at

www.Harlequin.com

HSRSM71795